SUDDEN SURRENDER

Mike Gannon's eyes narrowed to angry slits as he watched the voluptuous quiver of Moira's firm flesh under the sheer nightgown.

"If I can't have your love, I'll buy you," he sneered and tossed down ten ten-dollar bills. "Now show some life, girl. That's a lot of money to spend, even for a lady."

Mike caught her roughly to him, his hands assaulting her satin-smooth, voluptuous flesh.

Moira's resistance changed to immediate interest, then to frenzied wantonness. "Darling, darling," she whimpered. "I just stopped being a lady. I'm your harlot—your Canal Street woman. I am, I am!"

AUTHOR'S PROFILE

James Kendricks is the pseudonym of a well-known writer in the paperback field. He is the author of hundreds of magazine stories and 16 books.

He was born in Brooklyn, N. Y., and is the proud owner of an A.B. and LL.B. degree from St. John's University and St. John's University Law School. He has been admitted to practice law before the New York State Bar and the Federal Bar.

He has been writing stories and novels since 1938 and is the author of two current MONARCH BOOKS bestsellers entitled SHE WOULDN'T SURRENDER and BEYOND OUR PLEASURE.

THE WICKED, WICKED WOMEN

James Kendricks

*Author of SHE WOULDN'T SURRENDER
and BEYOND OUR PLEASURE*

WILDSIDE PRESS

FOREWORD

Canal Street was a birth pang of the city of Buffalo.

For many years it was known as one of the most wicked streets in the world, equivalent to the Barbary Coast of San Francisco, Dumaine Street of New Orleans, the Bowery of New York, Whitechapel of London, the Rue Pigalle of Paris.

Time throws a soft mantle over the wickedness which in another era was anathema to the good people of Buffalo. Today, Canal Street is but a memory. It lives only in the sere files of nineteenth century newspapers. Even the name is gone.

And yet—

There was a time when fights and murders were a daily occurrence along that quarter-mile. Policemen walked in threes to stay alive. More than half a thousand harlots plied their trade in so-called 'boarding houses'. Canal Street was an unhealthy seed flat where human nature was allowed to reveal its worst aspects.

Just as our frontier west endured an age of violence and bloodshed during its expansion, just as Ghana today is enduring it, so too with Canal Street. This explosive violence, with its attendant vice seems to be a part of human life, a necessary spiritual purge which mankind seems destined to endure so that from it may arise a new and better breed of men.

Unfortunately, there are few records of Canal Street to be consulted. No modern Boswell has set quill on paper to write of its terrors and temptations, its sins and iniquities.

5

Any history of the years between 1827 and 1901—which is the period when the Big Ditch street flourished—consists only of a notation here, a memory there. Its text cannot trace effect from cause, and the minutiae of the daily lives of those people who called it home are forever lost.

And so it is with the art of the novelist rather than that of the historian that I have attempted to bring Canal Street back to life for just a little while, seeing it through the eyes of an imaginary man and an imaginary woman, using fictional characters to act out the roles created by others.

James Kendricks

CHAPTER ONE

Mike Gannon leaped from the wooden dock onto the two men who stood with axe handles in their hands on the deck plankings of his barge, the *Lady Luck*. They heard the wind of his dive a second too late. As they turned he barreled into them, sending both of them sprawling across the deck. An axe handle went flying through the air. One man banged the hatchway coaming with the back of his head and lay unmoving.

Gannon lifted the second man off the deck boards with a hand on the lapels of his dark blue pea jacket. With his other hand clenched into a big fist, he drove it hard against the face before him. He heard the crunch of cartilage as his knuckles rammed a nose. His fist came back and struck again.

"You tell Black John Bennett to come himself next time he wants to put me out of business!"

His left hand opened and dropped the unconscious bargeman and now he whirled, seeing two more men coming up the few steps of the companionway, wicked belaying pins off a Great Lakes freighter in their fingers. They were grinning wolfishly at the sight of him, expecting easy prey.

Mike Gannon did not wait for their rush. He took two long steps and then he was before them, booted foot lifting to drive hard into the chest of one, slamming him backward into the hold while his other hand caught at the forearm of the second man, bringing it down hard across his knee. He had no time to think of niceties of conduct. Against two armed men and himself weaponless, he was concerned only with self-preservation.

Mike applied pressure to the forearm across his knee and the man screamed, "Jesus, man—let be! You'll break it."

"It's what I'm aiming to do, you fool!"

The man screamed again, thickly, his cry drowning out the sound of the snapping bone. Gannon lifted him and hurled him against the cabin wall. Then he was driving blindly down the companionway stairs into the blackness of the hold, expecting to feel the thudding impact of a belaying pin against his skull.

A red fury held him in its grip. He'd known for a long time that Black John Bennett was crowding out the other, smaller barge owners and canal captains. A raid of bully-boys, a broken skull or two, and your canawler was always ready to settle for a sale to Bennett Enterprises, usually at a loss to himself and at a fine margin of profit for Black John.

The Bennett empire was expanding, all along the Erie Canal.

Now Black John had put his mark on the Lucky Line and Captain Mike Gannon. Well, the hell with Black John! He'd throw his toughs right back in his face. Nobody got the Lucky Line. Nobody at all. He had built it up from one barge, five years before, right after Moira Kennally—damn her lovely eyes—had thrown him over for that rich bastard, Creegan—until now the Lucky Line stood second only to Black John's Empire Barges.

He poised in the darkness, crouched down, letting his eyes accustom themselves to the dimness of the hold. There was no belaying pin to his skull, nor rush of pounding feet. Whoever waited down here for him wanted all the odds in his favor, because he was afraid.

Mike Gannon chuckled to himself. Two could play at this game. He went forward lightly for all his two hundred pounds of solid bone and muscle, knowing this hold as he knew his own face. Here were the tanned leather goods out of Gloversville and over yonder the glassware from Corning. He could make out the crated machine parts from Albany and the bales of men's and women's wear from Troy.

A footfall sounded.

He whirled, instinctively knowing where to go. Now that his back was turned the roustabout would be making for the companionway stairs, having no stomach for a knockdown, drag-out fight with this man who'd already disposed of three of his companions.

He saw the man outlined against the sunlight in the hatchway opening, scrambling up the stairs, sobbing in fright. Mike launched himself in a diving tackle. His shoulder hit the man behind his knees, driving them viciously into a tread. His arms locked tight.

8

Rolling and thumping down the stairs, they hit the hold planks and now Gannon twisted like a big cat to pin his man down. His fist was a pile driver, lifting and falling. When the man beneath him slumped limply, he rose and shook himself. Reaching down, he tangled fingers in the thick mackinaw and dragged the man out onto the deck, dropping him like a sack of potatoes beside his unconscious fellows.

One by one he doused them with water from a bucket.

As a man stirred and sat up, Mike growled, "Tell Black John to come himself next time. Now what was it you were about to do to my *Lucky Lady?*"

"We rigged a nail keg of dynamite with a long fuse so she'd blow when we were well away from here," the man mumbled between mashed lips.

"A kind of bomb, then. All right. Come down in my hold, all of you, one at a time, nice and easy, and take your bomb away with you."

He gripped an axe handle himself now, and the four bullyboys eyed it warily as they walked ahead of him, moving slowly and afraid. Under his watchful stare they disconnected the fuse from the dynamite, handling it gingerly. Mike felt his flesh crawl at the sight of it. If that thing had gone up, his fine new barge would be a flaming ruin. Hate ran like a vein of acid in his body, but he controlled himself as one of the dock-wallopers tucked the keg under an arm and made for the companionway stairs.

Mike Gannon watched them go, knowing this was not the end of it, nor even the beginning. Black John would strike again. If that failed, he would keep hitting and trying until one day he had Mike Gannon where he wanted, a broken man, and the Lucky Line all for himself.

He drove the axe handle at a piling as he watched the four bullyboys walk away down Canal Street. Maybe he ought to gather a few of his own musclemen and pay Black John a visit, smash his nose or his teeth with one of his own axe handles. A fighting itch grew inside him—he wanted to feel flesh bruising under his fists.

"If I weren't going to Rome first thing in the morning in the *Lucky Penny*, I would."

Moira Kennally Creegan lived in Rome now. After five years he might get to see her. Thinking about black-haired Moira, a different kind of excitement began to build in

9

his blood. He sighed and dropped the axe handle, calling himself a fool.

The afternoon shadows were growing longer. Here and there in the saloons and honky-tonks gas lamps were coming on, throwing a yellow radiance into the twilight. A piano twinkled a light melody into the gathering darkness. Captain Mike Gannon turned his stare up the cobbled length of Canal Street. The most sinful street in the world, the folks north of the Liberty Pole in The Terrace said of it.

Up there, along Delaware Avenue and Main Street, were the respectable people of Buffalo, folks who thought Canal Street a crying shame and tried every once in a while to do something about it. Gannon guessed nobody could do very much. Even President Grover Cleveland—when he'd been sheriff of Erie County back in the '70s—had failed to wipe out Big Ditch Street. It would need a mighty big eruption to do that, he supposed.

Canal Street averaged a dozen fights a night, one murder every other night. The good people of the city secretly hoped there'd come a night when everybody down here would murder everybody else so decent society could come in and clean it up.

"I'll never live to see the day," he philosophized.

Just the same, Canal Street had been good to him. His first barge had multiplied to three and then five. At this moment he owned ten, and had upwards of eighty men on his payroll. He had made a name for the Lucky Line up and down the canal. Only John Bennett's Empire Barges was a larger outfit than his own.

He shoved hands deep into his pea jacket pockets and turned away from the canal, past the wooden pilings, stepping over refuse and garbage as he went. A wonder folks along the canal didn't all die of disease, with all this filth lying around. A huge gray rat clung to a bit of rotted meat, its beady eyes fastened on him boldly.

The sky was darkening rapidly. Gas lamps began to glow a little brighter. Three sailors off one of the Great Lakes freighters came weaving down the street, arm in arm. One of the sailors saw him and cupped a hand to his mouth.

"No money, canawler?"

Gannon grinned and waved an arm. There was always an uneasy truce when a canal man met a Great Lakes sailor.

10

A word or an untimely laugh could turn that meeting into a bloody brawl. More than one fight had found him in its middle, driving huge fists into faces or bellies, roaring with the sheer joy of battle.

The sailors went on past the Tub of Blood, hunting another place. Gannon wondered where they would spend the night. In the Golconda? The Federal? There were a hundred saloons, a hundred honky-tonks, to cater to their needs.

They might even be dead come morning.

A light went on in an upper room across the street. A woman stood framed in the window, looking down at him. She wore a black corselet tight around her middle, above which smooth breasts gleamed like marble. Long brown hair fell about her shoulders. She looked like an Oriental concubine posing in European garments.

As she saw him staring, she laughed and blew a kiss. A moment longer she posed for him before touching a cord and causing the heavy maroon drapes to swish across the window, hiding herself and the room behind her.

Captain Gannon discovered that he had stopped walking to gawk. He shook himself angrily. Certainly he knew how a woman looked in her undergarments! Yet there had been an animality about this unknown female which had reached out and choked the breath in his throat.

His gaze lowered from the window to study the large house with its gingerbread scrollwork on porch roof and pillars. A sign across the way said: THE MUMMY CASE. From what he could see of the interior—a flash of gilded woodwork near the ceiling and part of a mirror above a bar —this was a cut above the ordinary saloons of the street. He wondered if the woman in the window was an entertainer. If so, she might be available for a few drinks and a night in a cubicle bed.

He told himself not to be guided by the sight of a bosom seen in gaslight for a few seconds, but even as he argued with himself his heavy leather bluchers were moving across the street flaggings toward The Mummy Case. Certainly his throat was dry. It would do no harm to down a glass of Irish whiskey.

A player piano was pounding out *The Wheelbarrow Polka* as the glass-paneled doors swung inward to his hand. A life-sized statue of a nude woman had been converted into a torchère to light the hallway with twin lanterns upheld in its hands. A bell tinkled somewhere in the far recesses of the building. The captain removed his peaked cap and pushed his way into the barroom, noting with surprise that the decorations were so well cared for—the mahogany bar polished to brightness and the giltwork of the chandeliers and wall brackets glistening spotlessly.

The beamed ceiling was smudged from years of cigar and pipe smoke. A thin layer of sawdust covered the floor. Brass spittoons and a long rail added a touch of color to the dark bar wood. Behind its eighty-foot length extended several long mirrors and the oil painting of a nude.

Aproned bartenders were polishing glasses and arranging bottles of Early Times and Hennessey's in pyramids at intervals along the bar. One of them turned and nodded at the free-lunch counter.

The barkeep said, "Smart to eat now while you can take your time. Might be you'll like our stage show, too. She puts on a good one, The Egyptian does."

"The Egyptian?"

"Name of the lady what runs the place." Mike's eyes rolled upward as the aproned man lifted his thumb. "Lives upstairs, right above here. Getting dressed just about now, I'd say."

The Egyptian. The woman in the window?

His hand closed around the shot glass and he drank the liquor down in one swallow. He moved to the free-lunch counter, selecting a hot corned beef sandwich and a couple of hard-boiled eggs. He ate slowly, resting his weight on his elbows at the bar. From time to time he would drain the beer mug placed before him.

Mike Gannon was a big man with a big appetite. He ate four sandwiches and six eggs in a little more than half an hour, together with half a pint of whiskey and close to a quart of beer. When he paused to throw down two dollar bills, his eyes touched a section of the huge curving staircase at the far end of the room.

A woman was coming down those carpeted treads.

She wore a Polonaise gown of striped piqué, with the upper skirt draped and looped over a gored underskirt. Her ankles were slim, decked out in clocked black silk stockings, revealed as her skirt swept back to her every downward step. The striped piqué gripped her hips like skin and showed a slim waist rising into a full bosom. Her shoulders and arms were bared to the gaslight.

12

Captain Gannon straightened slowly. She was regarding him with thin eyebrows arched, a faint smile on her wide red mouth. No doubt about it. This was the woman who had blown him a kiss from her bedroom window.

"Joe," she called. "Bring my dinner. And ask the captain if he cares to join me."

Without another glance, she moved down the stairs and across the back of the room to a table. The long saloon formed an ell at this point, the short end becoming a tiny theater for the curtained stage. Tables and chairs had been set up here, where the sailors and bargemen could take their ease and enjoy the shows.

A bartender brought a plate filled with steaming corned beef, boiled potatoes and a wedge of cabbage. Captain Gannon found himself moving forward to hold the chair for her.

"I saw you standing on the street, didn't I, Captain?" she asked, letting him slide the chair under her.

"You did that. It's why I came in here."

"You flatter me, Captain Gannon. As a Canal Street woman I'm not used to flattery." Her hand lifted. "Joe, bring the captain a drink. He's a rare visitor. Perhaps we can make him a steady customer."

Her face was broad, with a ripely sensual mouth and a wide forehead above which brown hair had been coiffed into a high-crowned upsweep. Her ears were tiny, her nose straight, her eyes large and intensely brown. The color of her skin was dusty, almost a *café-au-lait,* giving her a foreign, exotic look, and the manner in which her smooth brown shoulders rose upward out of the low collar of her evening gown suggested that the body beneath it might be as challenging and as exciting as the face itself. At the moment her eyes were brilliant under the mascara and blue eye paste, bold and challenging. A faint touch of hardness showed itself in the lines at the corners of her vividly outlined mouth and in the sardonic arch of her plucked eyebrows. He judged her to be in her early thirties.

"Looking for fun, Captain?"

"If I am, have I found it?"

She considered that, head tilted sideways as she ate. Mike Gannon found her a very attractive woman. The memory of her large breasts was still fresh in his mind. The thought came to him that he had been a long time without a woman in his arms, and that sometimes a man was a fool to devote his every waking moment to business. He moved a little

13

in his chair and found his knee against her thigh. She did not move from the contact.

The Egyptian had been eating steadily. Now she glanced at him sideways and put down her knife and fork. "You said that like a challenge."

"Maybe I meant it as a challenge."

"When I was a little younger, Captain, I was never one to refuse a dare. Seems that's what you're doing right now —daring me."

"And if I were?"

Her eyes narrowed slightly. "I don't use the entertainers' rooms, Captain. By that I mean I don't sell myself to— ordinary customers. Man wants me, he has to come right out and tell me so."

She stood up abruptly, kicking back the chair. "I have work to do. I don't let anything interfere with that. If you're still here by midnight, I'll see you again."

She swept away, the Polonaise gown rustling to her stride. Under that striped piqué her hips moved evenly, gracefully. Either she was firmly fleshed down there or she was wearing a corset. Captain Gannon chuckled. Might be fun to find that out for himself, come a few minutes after midnight.

His hand lifted and a bartender slipped around the edge of the bar toward him. Half a dozen men were lined up over the brass rail now, starting the evening off with straight rye. In an hour The Mummy Case would be filling up.

"Joe, if I order tonight, water down my drink. I'll pay you the same rates as for straight stuff. I just don't want my thinking to get too fuzzy."

Gannon rose and stretched, the food and liquor warm in his middle. Out of the corner of his eye he saw three big men come through the door. The man who walked a little ahead of the others was Black John Bennett. He wondered if Bennett was hunting him. Moving toward the little stage, Mike Gannon pursed his lips thoughtfully, crossed to the wall and wrenched loose the thick leg of a chair. He tucked the makeshift club up his trousered leg as he sat down. It never hurt a man to be ready for trouble.

Seated at his little table, sipping his watered whiskey slowly, he waited for discovery. Would Bennett come with a roaring curse and flailing fists? No, probably not. Bennett fancied himself a respectable man. He sent his dock-wallopers out on the dirty jobs—to burn the barges and crack the skulls of the men who dared to stand up to him—

14

while he himself sat in a nice clean office, usually in a white shirt and with a tie on.

Tonight he was slumming. Or it just might be that he was out to finish off Mike Gannon. Those two men with him were hulking brutes, muscular and powerful, with hard, savage faces, wearing turtle-neck sweaters and blue mackinaws. The best of his bullyboys? Mike grinned coldly. Black John would need them if he started trouble.

Black John Bennett was as big a man as Gannon, but he was given to putting on weight so that he seemed much heavier. There was a puffiness about his hard black eyes and a bluish sheen to his shaven cheeks. He wore a checkered vest strung with a gold watch chain from which swung a gleaming five-dollar gold piece like a banner to announce his coming. His clothes were clean and carefully pressed, his frock coat with high lapels thrown back negligently to show the coin watch charm. He came between the tables as men drew back before him, glancing at him, then turning to whisper to their neighbors.

There was an arrogance about the man that drove splinters of fury into Mike Gannon. His hand itched to swing the chair leg; still, he told himself, he'd not be the one to start trouble here, despite what had happened on the *Lady Luck* a little earlier. And so he drew back further into the shadows and waited.

The room was filling rapidly now. The aproned waiters ran this way and that with trays and, periodically, a bartender would scurry over with Mike's watered special so he might keep his throat wet while he watched the show. He had waved away the man who'd come with a long candle pole to light the gas mantle at his back. Now he sat almost in darkness, shadowed by the angle of the stair landing.

Black John had not seen him yet.

He would soon enough, however. He was approaching with his henchmen at his elbows. Mike tensed and put a hand on the broken chair leg, ready to yank it loose from under his trousers. None of the three men so much as glanced in his direction. Slowly he relaxed.

This was no place for a meeting between them. A meeting would come, but at a time and in a manner of his own choosing, Mike told himself. He would demand his accounting from Bennett when and where he willed, not where destiny thrust it on him. He was no hot-tempered youngster to go off like a half-cocked pistol.

The lights began to dim as the bar waiters went around to the wall fixtures. A piano sounded a few bars and the room grew still. The music was lively and gay; probably French, thought Gannon.

Heavy maroon drapes swept back, revealing the painted backdrop of a Parisian street with the Eiffel Tower in the distance. The piano quickened its tempo and a line of girls came prancing out onto the boards. They wore short red skirts with tightly fitted bodices and high black silk stockings with red pumps. Gannon guessed they were supposed to be from Paris. A sign on an easel on a corner of the stage read *The French Can-Can*.

Silken legs flashed up in a high kick.

The crowd roared at the sight of white thighs, black stockings and pink garters. The girls kicked again and again, and between times would balance on one leg and rotate the other at the knee. They wore lacy white panties. Even Captain Gannon stared, not quite remembering the last time he'd seen so many female limbs.

The girls kicked and cavorted, laughing at the excited yells that greeted their every display, their faces flushed and eyes bright above heavily painted lips. Their shoulders were bare, as were their arms. Gannon thought them a good cut above the usual performers Canal Street offered.

Evidently Black John Bennett did, too. He stirred and muttered, "Me, I'd take the blonde on this end if I was to have a choice."

"Why don't you, sir? We'll give you a hand," said one tough.

"Who's to stop us?" rumbled the other. "A crowd of bums and a couple of toffs from north of the Terrace? You take your blonde. I'll grab that little redhead. Toad here can take whoever catches his eye. We'll take them to the rooms over Shaughnessy's Bar."

Black John needed little persuasion. He thrust back his chair and got to his feet. As he did so, Mike Gannon yanked out his broken chair leg.

Gannon rose, the chair leg gripped in a big hand. He stepped around the table and swung.

The chair leg hit the Irishman's thick skull and bounced, splitting. For a moment Black John stood erect, a shudder running through his broad back, then down into his legs. Then with a little sigh, he pitched forward on his face.

His companions had started toward the stage. Now they

16

turned back, seeing Bennett sprawled across the table. Their eyes went to the smiling barge captain, widening with shock and disbelief.

"Looks like he had too much to drink," Gannon said agreeably. "Better get him out of here fast."

Only the waiters had seen the by-play but they were moving away from the walls now, with the bung starters they always kept hidden in trouser pockets naked in their fists. The two bullyboys looked as if they might start swinging but Black John lay slumped unconscious at their feet. Without a leader, they were lost. They were used to following orders and no orders were forthcoming.

One of them shrugged. "Come on, Toad. Let's get Bennett out. We can always settle matters with Gannon another time."

The men bent and lifted Bennett, carrying him under his armpits so that his heavy brogans dragged along the sawdust floor. Few men in the audience bothered to look away from the stage where the girls were now high-kicking more lustily than ever.

Gannon sat down and reached for his glass. Even as he saw it was empty, a ringed hand replaced it with a full bottle of whiskey.

"For a job well done, Captain," smiled The Egyptian.

She slipped into a nearby chair and leaned elbows on the tabletop. She nodded her head at the tables around them. "You saved me a lot of money by that prompt action. There'd have been a beautiful free-for-all if you hadn't. I keep twenty waiters here for trouble like that but it's hard to prevent it from getting started. Once it starts the place gets wrecked. I've had to redecorate five times in the last three years." She made a face. "It costs money, a lot of money, to redecorate on Canal Street. Not many carpenters and painters are willing to work down here."

"Forget what I did," he told her, pouring for her and for himself. "I had to break a chair to do it."

"I'll bill Black John for that. He'll pay me, too, next time he's in here and sober."

"I'm Irish myself," grinned Mike, "but Black John's a disgrace to the race. I'll bet a cookie he's from Ulster."

She laughed and swallowed. Mike let his eye touch her soft throat and lower to the crease between her large breasts.

"You said to tell you," he grinned, putting a palm to her

upper thigh so the clasp of her garter was under his fingers. "I'm admitting it now. I want you. I never thought I'd want any other woman but Moira Kennally, but she's been married five years and five years can be the devil of a long time for a healthy man, believe me."

"Wait just a little while," she whispered, leaning closer to touch his hand with hers, smiling roguishly. "I count my receipts at one o'clock. You can help me."

When she thrust the bottle at him he pushed it away with a wry grin. "When I'm drinking I don't want a woman near me. When I'm wenching I hate the sight of a bottle."

Her hand closed on his fingers, held them tightly. The brilliance of her eyes under their blued lids sent a glow throughout his body.

They talked in low tones while the stage offered its girl dancers and singers. Three aproned waiters sang *The Charming Young Widow I Met on the Train,* while a pretty redhead as the widow, and a brunette beauty as the gullible traveler, pantomimed the verses. A roar of delight went up while the redheaded widow neatly removed the traveler's watch and chain and somehow caused the trousers to fall, revealing the brunette beauty in silk stockings and transparent underdrawers.

Mike Gannon and The Egyptian heard little of what went on around them. He had started the dusky woman to talking about her early life and paid her the compliment of silence.

"My mother was a cook on a canal barge. Mother Casey rented her out to the captains. Somewhere along the Erie I was conceived. I never knew who my father was, except that he was a canawler. Maybe my mother didn't know, either. She was rented out to a lot of them, she told me.

"She died of tuberculosis when I was eleven. Mother Casey brought me up. When I was fifteen she rented me out, too, but I wasn't having any of the kind of life my mother led, thank you. I saved my money. I bought into The Mummy Case when Otis Coleman owned it. They called it The Coal Scuttle then."

Her smooth shoulders lifted in a casual shrug. "One day a drunk came in and began shooting up the place. Otis tried to take his gun away and got a bullet in his middle for his pains. He died in my arms over there at the end of the bar.

"The police came at the run at the first shot. They caught the drunk as he ran out onto the cobblestones and

18

hustled him off in the paddy wagon to the Franklin Avenue police station. They hung him a year later. Nobody ever found out why he did it. Maybe he was just crazy from cheap rotgut booze.

"Anyway, I suppose you'd say he did me a favor. Maybe he did. There was nobody but me to take over The Coal Scuttle. I redecorated it, called it The Mummy Case, added the Egyptian motif, called myself The Egyptian."

"What's your real name?" he wondered.

Her pouting mouth twisted into a smile. "Does it make any difference? I'm just an illusion, a way to make a man forget."

She rose to her feet, stood swaying, looking down at him. His eyes ran over the swell of her thighs against the tight piqué, up around the gentle mound of belly to the jutting breasts. Her mouth was curving almost tenderly as she whispered down at him.

"Come along, Captain. I know a lot of ways to rub out a man's memory. Treat me real good and maybe I'll use a few of them on you."

Mike Gannon went after her swinging hips, past the tables crowded with men, into a smaller room fitted with a roll-top desk and a chair, a small table heavy with books and a wooden file cabinet. Half a dozen canvas money sacks had been thrown on the desk, beyond which was a squat Corbin safe.

The Egyptian gestured casually. "Make yourself at home, Captain. There are cigars in the humidor. I won't be long."

Mike struck a match, holding it to the Corona clamped between his teeth, studying the woman as she bent above the sacks, upending them, flooding the roll-top desk with bills and coins. She reached for a ledger. She was competent and efficient when it came to money, he saw. No tomfoolery about her then, and no awareness of her ripe body.

He blew smoke, enjoying the rich taste of the Havana tobacco, hearing only the scratching of the pen with which she made her entries and notations. He was a little surprised at the amount of money she was counting. He'd thought he owned a flourishing business along the canal; it was peanuts compared to the revenue of The Mummy Case.

"I'm in the wrong line," he told her with a chuckle.

Her smile was preoccupied. "Men will always pay hard cash for a good time, Captain. I furnish the good time, they furnish the cash."

19

She made two more notations, then threw down the pen.

"There! I'm done." Her bare arms lifted high above her head as she wriggled her fingers and then interlocked them, smiling with sultry invitation at the canawler. There was a faint hair stubble in her armpits, which he found more stimulating than shaven skin.

He tossed aside the cigar and took a long step forward. His hands went to her slim waist, lifting her up out of the chair, bringing her against him. Her mouth was soft and loose, taking his kiss with an honest hunger.

The barge captain slid his palms down her back to her hips, holding her firmly until he felt her bare arms about his neck, clinging fiercely. Against his lips she whispered, "It hasn't been five years for me, Mike Gannon, but it wasn't yesterday, either."

"Where?" he asked hoarsely.

"The back door. There's a private stairway walled off from the rest of the house. I use it sometimes to work late at night, when I don't want to dress up."

He carried her with one arm over her soft thighs and with her rump resting on a shoulder, listening to her laughter as she ducked when he opened the back-stairs door so they could go under the lintel. He carried her up the stairs and along a narrow corridor.

She reached down and turned a brass knob.

The room before them was heavy with Victorian furniture. Lace antimacassars covered the arms and backs of overstuffed chairs and sofa. A beaded curtain shut off a bedroom from the reading room into which he carried her, to deposit her, with a revelation of shapely stockinged legs, on the wide Belter sofa.

An ormolu clock stood on the marble mantelpiece, flanked by a copy of the bronze statue of *Salammbo* by Jerome and a bronze replica of Stephan Sinding's *Kiss of Adoration*. A thick Turkish carpet was underfoot, and close to the white ceiling an ornately carved and gilded cornice was hung with a scalloped fabric called swag. The drapes were tied back with silken ropes and oversized tassels. Captain Gannon stared around him a moment.

"You do yourself proud," he murmured wryly. "I've not seen a better decorated drawing room in any of the houses I've been in, all along The Big Ditch."

The Egyptian stretched, writhing her legs and hips on the edge of the couch as he stared at her. "I like nice things. I don't mind paying for them. When I was a little girl and saw my mother go off to cook and such for some bearded barge captain, leaving me to a bare, unheated room with only broken furniture and not enough covers on the bed at night, I swore I'd have plenty of everything when I grew up. And I have."

She held up her hands, let him pull her to a sitting position. Even while he stood staring, her fingers went to the hairpins and combs in her thick brown hair, tugging them free, loosening the thick strands so that her hair fell loose and dangling over her shoulders.

The Egyptian turned her back, sitting on the edge of the sofa, knees close together. "Unfasten me, darling. I sent Poppy home two hours ago. Poppy's my maid."

Mike chuckled as he undid a hook and eye, and then another. "You were mighty confident of me, weren't you? Well, you have reason to be. You're a damned attractive woman."

His mouth touched her shoulder where it met her throat, finding it warm and smooth. His lips ran down her bared back to the edge of her short black corselet. In front, her hands held the piqué bodice to her otherwise naked breasts.

"Anxious, Mike?" she whispered.

His hands slipped under the bodice to hold her heavy breasts. At the touch of the sleek, soft flesh, his breath caught in his throat. "As anxious as a schoolboy. Now stand up like a good girl and step out of that fine gown you're only half wearing."

The Egyptian laughed softly and twisted free of him. Impishness mixed with sensuality in her face as she took a few steps away from the sofa where he sat. The gown was falling from her shoulders where the long brown hair hung so thickly. One side of it was held in a hand, exposing her leg from bared thigh down the length of her stockinged leg to a red evening pump. She looked very much the eager, sensual woman to Captain Gannon at the moment.

He found himself in no mood to play games. An excitement was geysering inside him, fed by the sight of this half-undressed woman posing so teasingly before him, playing him like a fisherman with a trout. Well, by God! No woman could treat him so!

His hand stabbed out to hook behind a stockinged knee, pulling her off balance so that she fell forward, squealing in

21

surprise. Then she was on top of him in her perfumed laces and satins and he felt the pressure of a bare shoulder against his mouth even as his palm stroked upward along her thigh.

When she opened her mouth to protest he turned her so that she lay half on and half off the divan, and then he kissed her, driving his lips onto hers, mashing them open to accept the entry of his tongue. Her fist swung against his shoulder but he never felt it. It was good to have woman-flesh in his arms again, crushed helpless to his muscles. His hand moved along her inner thigh and he felt her body go tense, then loosen as a low moan grew in her throat.

The arms that had fought him closed around him. She arched herself upward with both high-buttoned shoes planted firmly on the carpet, urging her hips toward him. With his left hand he tore at the black corselet, stripping it down and away from her breasts.

For an instant he stared at those firm mounds studded with rigid scarlet nipples, then his head was bending and his lips went searching. He could hear the hiss of her in-drawn breath, the crooning voice that whispered words at him, urging him on, whipping his senses with panted obscenities.

"Take me, Mike. This way, here on the couch. Later maybe we'll use the bed but right now—"

He did what she asked and what he wanted to do, brutally and like an animal, but his very animality was an excitation that whipped her to a frenzy. She screamed thinly in his ear again and again before her teeth closed on his shoulder.

CHAPTER TWO

White clouds raced across a blue sky as the *Lucky Penny* sliced its watery way past Rochester and headed for the long run to Rome. Mike Gannon stood at the tiller of his hundred-foot barge, eyes moving along the taut towlines where two mules dug iron hooves into the dirt towpath, urged along by his driver.

His consignment stop was the city of Rome, New York,

where he was to pick up and transport to Buffalo a load of iron ingots refined by the Creegan Iron Works. Richard Creegan owned those foundries. His wife was Moira Kennally Creegan.

The Creegan Iron Works would pay well. In one sense it was a stroke of luck, his getting the business. He could not avoid the thought that Moira might be responsible for it. To handle all Richard Creegan's consignments would make him a rich man in eight or nine years. He wondered if Moira would be in the foundry offices when he appeared for his cargo.

He wanted her to be there, with all his heart.

Another part of him understood that it would be foolish for her to appear just so he could feast his eyes on her face once again. It would only reopen old wounds, even after five long years. He might as well face the fact. He would never get that black-haired beauty out of his system. Not even The Egyptian could help him do that.

Oh, she had been wild and wanton after their session on the couch, just the way he liked a woman to be, parading around the bedroom in her black corselet above which her breasts had jumped and jiggled, rich thighs banded by black garters—letting him see all he wanted of her, commanding him to remain glued to the spot where he stood after helping her off with her undergarments, making him watch as she touched a perfume dropper to her armpits, to the straining brown buds of her big breasts.

Until he was roused to madness by the sight of her nakedness, until he tore the wrapper with which she sought to cover herself from her hands and threw her down on the counterpane. Laughing, she had fought him until the frenzy worked in her own blood and then she had opened herself to him with a sob and a high, shrill cry . . .

A passing barge almost grazed his stern. Captain Gannon snapped awake, veering his tiller slightly. Be smarter to keep his mind on his business than to go remembering those hectic hours last night. The new barge responded instantly, as if a giant hand had reached out to thrust it off to starboard.

Quite a contrast between his new *Lucky Penny* and the old barge which his father had named *Luck o' the Irish*. In those days he had walked the towpaths behind a brace of gray mules, switch in hand and bare toes digging into the soft loam of the towpath, trailing the hooves of the mules

23

as the long chains and frayed leather harness tightened to their drag.

It had been his job to guide the mules—those fifteen years before—while his father stayed on the barge. He often thought his feet had worn a rut all across New York State, from Albany to Buffalo. He could still see the shiny flanks of Mouse and Graybeard as the muscles bunched and shifted under their glossy hides. Time was, he had been sick of the sight and smell of mule-flesh. Now he breathed in clean fresh air while a helper walked with the towlines.

His hand touched the side pocket of his pea jacket. A crackle of paper sounded—his consignment sheet for the iron he was to take aboard at the Rome docks. And Moira Creegan lived in Rome.

He ought to go see her, just for old times' sake. Rich Mister Creegan could hardly object if he paid his wife a friendly visit. She ought to know he was alive and well and doing nicely, thank you.

Mike Gannon began to whistle a merry tune.

Moira Creegan straightened abruptly and let the heavy window drape slide into place with a faint rustle of damask. She put her hands to her cheeks and drew a deep breath, feeling strangely excited. Could she believe her eyes? For an instant she shook her head and told herself she should not have taken that glass of blackberry brandy after lunch.

Her hand went out to the drapes and pushed them back a second time. Her gaze fastened on the figure of the tall man walking so confidently up the tree-lined avenue toward the house. There could be no doubt now. It was Mike—big Mike Gannon!

"Oh, Mike—you silly fool," she whispered. "I thought I'd seen the last of you five years ago when I married Richard."

She felt elation surge through her, and a tiny touch of fear. Mike had never forgotten her. He was still in love with her. Now he was defying all rules and coming to see her. What would Richard say to that?

Moira ran to the hatrack in the lower front hall, lifting trembling fingers to her thick black hair, primping a little, seeing a pale white face with wide and long-lashed eyes, an overfull mouth that seemed perpetually red, and carefully plucked brows. Her girlhood beauty had matured and ripened in the past five years.

24

Her palms slid down her sides to her hips. In the pale blue foulard afternoon dress she looked the part of a pretty young matron, the mother of a girl four years old. No one would ever guess she was not the happy wife she seemed. The foulard was only one of many gowns and dresses that crowded her upstairs closets, for Richard insisted that she dress in the very latest fashions. But it took more than new dresses to make a woman bubble with delight, as she was bubbling now, with just one glimpse of big Mike coming up the sidewalk.

A bell tinkled far back in the kitchen.

"I'm here, Bertha," she called. "I'll take it."

Her heart was slamming under the squared bodice as she forced herself to walk slowly to the front door. Through the lacework covering the big glass panel she could see Mike standing with his face turned half away as he stared down Depeyster Street. Her hand closed almost convulsively on the doorknob.

"Mike," she cried, "Mike Gannon!"

"Hello, Moira." His eyes touched her face and she could read the hungry wanting in them. She opened the door wider.

"Come in. This certainly is a surprise."

He brought a touch of the outdoors. His broad shoulders and long legs moving gracefully, hinting at the powerfully muscled body under the blue pea jacket and turtle-neck sweater. His captain's cap was in one hand and the afternoon sunlight formed a golden halo around his head before the door closed to shut it out.

"They told me at the basin I might find your husband here," he said slowly. "I have a consignment of iron ingots to ship to Buffalo for him. There's some confusion over how many are to go."

"I've been expecting him all afternoon. We were supposed to attend a tea at two o'clock. It's after three now. He still hasn't come home. Come into the parlor, Mike. I'll ask Bertha to bring some tea and cake. Or would you like something stronger?"

"Tea and cake is fine," he nodded.

They were strangers, ill at ease with one another. Mike sat on the edge of an ornate, overstuffed wing chair with his cap half crushed in long fingers. Moira moved to and from the heavily draped windows. Her legs were weak and trembling. She told herself not to be a fool. Once she and Mike Gannon had been in love. Their love affair had broken up long ago.

"Still got the *Lucky Charm?*" she asked suddenly.

"Sure. Bought nine more barges since those days."

"You're doing well, then. I'm glad, Mike."

His hand made a vague gesture. "I'll never do as well as this. Guess you knew that when you married Creegan." He asked as casually as he could. "You happy with him, Moira? I mean, has it been all you wanted it to be?"

Her lips quivered and for a moment she was afraid she was going to cry; then some of her old toughness came into her voice. "Now what do you think, Mike Gannon? Was I raised to live in a place like this, with people who look down their noses at me for not being one of their own kind? Could any girl be happy?"

He was staring at her, eyes wide, his jaw fallen open. She said harshly, "I'm not good enough for his sisters and his cousins—oh, the whole kit and kaboodle of them. Maybe I could stomach them if Richard weren't so much the businessman and more the—you know what I mean," she finished lamely.

"Jesus, I never thought—"

"I had to go back to school, mind you. To learn to speak correctly, to learn something about history and books and how to eat properly and conduct myself as a lady. A lady! My father was a dock-walloper off a Great Lakes steamer. My mother was a cook in a Fly Street restaurant."

She drew a deep breath and crossed the room, yanking at a pull cord. Moments later a slim woman in maid's uniform entered and curtseyed.

"Bertha, this is Captain Gannon. Would you make a pot of tea? And are there any of those gingerbread cookies left?"

"I'll see, mum."

When the maid was gone and they were alone the silence of the room seemed to close in around them, broken only by the faint ticking of the upright clock in a corner of the hall. The parlor was stiffly formal with overstuffed sofa and ottoman and a marble-topped table on which rested a glass dome encasing an arrangement of wax flowers. The formality of the room transferred itself to its uneasy occupants. Twice Moira surprised his quick, almost furtive glances at her.

26

Mike muttered, "Maybe I ought to run along. I can see your husband tomorrow at the foundry."

"Not yet," she countered suddenly, dreading to see him walk out of her life a second time. Her hand lifted as if she would hold him in the chair by sheer force. Her tongue moistened her lips. "Bertha's bringing tea, Mike. I—I've never seen a barge man drinking tea."

He grinned and she laughed, and suddenly they felt more at ease. Mike dropped his cap to the floor at his feet while his hand indicated his heavy woolen sweater and jacket. "I feel mighty out of place here. Guess you know that."

"You think I don't? Richard's sisters make me feel completely unwanted. At first it wasn't too bad, with Richard a bridegroom, but now it's getting worse every day. Sometimes I feel just like packing up and running away from everything. Maybe I would, too, if it weren't for my little girl."

"It isn't all you thought it'd be then, is it?" he asked harshly, unable to resist the taunt. Seeing her in the crisp day gown with her thick black hair done up so neatly in a low chignon was a powerful reminder that he'd never get another chance with Moira Kennally. "If you'd been content to start small—"

"Ah, must you remind me of it?" she flashed, cheeks flushed. "And what about yourself, Mike Gannon? I turned you down and no sooner were the words cold on my lips than you had that doxy off Canal Street snug in your barge cabin, half undressed and almost drunk."

"That's what's eating in your craw, is it? Just because I'm a man with a man's hungers, you throw it up to me."

"Mike Gannon, you're a black gossoon. It wasn't over the doxy we quarreled and well you know it. All I ever asked of you was to get off the canal. To go into an office and wear decent clothes when you came home nights to dinner."

"The canal is all I know," he growled.

"All you want to know!"

They were standing almost nose to nose, with big Mike bending down and Moira on tiptoe, the better to snap at him. Forgotten was the front parlor with its overstuffed furniture, its heavy window draperies and gold-framed oil paintings. During a pause in their harsh breathing they heard the maid approaching, pushing a tea cart ahead of her; they drew apart, Gannon walking toward a window

27

to stare blindly out at the street, Moira to pour Bohea from the sterling silver teapot into delicate Wedgewood cups. The maid went down the hall and to the kitchen.

"Mike, the tea is ready," she said.

"Tea," he snorted. "I'd rather have a thimble of Irish whiskey."

"I'd expect nothing else of you," she snapped. There was a quaver in her voice and tears in her eyes.

"Ah, now, *acushla*—"

"I can't help it, Mike. I'm just—miserable."

He came to put his arms about her, drawing her against him, letting her sob on his chest. "The night we quarreled—when you went off to find that blond tart and I followed you—was the night I said yes to Richard. I was furious at you, Mike—simply furious."

She wept a little, remembering. "I thought it would all be roses and moonlight, being a rich man's wife. I didn't realize that a rich man would have a family—and that he might have a mistress or two."

"Mistresses? When he's got you?"

She smiled through her tears. Her hand came up to caress his cheek. "Why were we always fighting? Why couldn't I have been happy with you the way you were?"

"Sure, I was only an overgrown yahoo—"

"We'd have been happy. I know that now. But it's too late. Too late, Mike."

He cleared his throat, suddenly aware that he was holding this woman so tight in his arms he could feel the solid thrust of her firm breasts and the softness of her hips where they pressed into him. It took a definite effort of will to push her back and away. "I'd best be going-before I forget myself," he chuckled.

"Mike, I—"

What Moira Creegan might have said was forgotten before the sound of the front door opening and the patter of running feet.

"Mommy, Mommy!" a child's voice yelled.

A little girl in cambric dress and black stockings ran from the hall into the parlor. Mike stood up and the child halted while her eyes grew round as she glanced from the strange man to her mother.

"This is Captain Gannon, darling. Mike, this is my daughter, Kathleen."

28

Mike smiled and held out a huge hand. "Sure, it's a pleasure, Kathleen. You're as pretty as your mother."

"You think my mommy's pretty?"

"I sure do. Don't you?"

Kathleen nodded solemnly and put up her hand for Mike to hold a moment, before going behind her mother and peering up at him past the full skirt which so effectively shielded her.

Mike said, "As long as I'm standing, I'll keep right on walking, Moira."

Moira Creegan accompanied him to the front door, with little Kathleen trailing after her. Standing with her left hand on the door and her eyes following the swing of his shoulders as he went down Depeyster Street and so on out of her life, Moira heard her heart cry out, *Come back again, Mike! Come back to me!* She bit down hard on her lip to still the aroused pounding of her blood. After a moment she was able to let the door close very gently.

An hour later she learned her husband had died.

Richard Ames Creegan was buried in a driving rainstorm on the first day of May, 1885. His widow stood with bowed head as the mahogany casket was being lowered into the grave in fashionable Mount Olive Cemetery, heedless of the water drumming on the umbrella held over her head by a sobbing Bertha.

From time to time, Aunt Martha Creegan let her eyes slide sideways at this woman who had been the wife of her wealthy brother. Her thin, lined face was filled with vindictive hate and resentment. *Fortune hunter! Adventuress!* Now the fabulously successful iron works belonged, not to the Creegan family, but to this woman Richard had lifted from the gutter.

Beside Martha Creegan, her two nephews stood with bowed heads. The older, Jason Evans Tomkins, was general manager of the Creegan Iron Works. Short and running to flesh, he could only think, *There goes my security, my job. Moira will run the foundry into the ground now. Still, might be I could salvage something by going to her, asking to be made president in Uncle Richard's place. If she knows anything at all about business, she'll be only too happy to let me run things for her.*

The younger nephew, Mark Tomkins, was still a student

29

at Cornell University. He had been promised that upon graduation he would have a good job in the foundry. Now he supposed that job was up the flue, buried the way Uncle Richard was being buried.

"It's time to go, Mum," said Bertha, nudging Moira with an elbow.

"What? Oh. Oh, yes."

Reality came back to Moira Creegan slowly. She could feel the water seeping into her thin kid shoes and running down her heavy dolman cape. Her face lifted and she noticed the hatred in the faces of Aunt Martha and cousins Jason and Mark. The boy's mother, Elvira Martin Tomkins, was clinging tearfully to her husband's arm, shaking her head back and forth, not bothering to show her hate as visibly as the others.

They expect me to fire the boys and throw Aunt Martha out of her fine home on Washington Street, and pull Frederick Tomkins' job out from under his feet. They've always feared and hated me, ever since Richard announced that he was going to marry me. I never did one thing to make them dislike me. Now that everything belongs to me they seem to feel I've turned into some kind of monster. They ought to come buttering me up, instead of showing their resentment so plainly.

A hand was under her elbow. "Dear Aunt Moira," said young Mark. "Let me help you over the puddles."

So it was beginning. She fought back the ironic smile and said softly. "Thank you, Mark. It's good to have a strong arm on which to lean."

"You can lean on all of us," Mark said quickly. "We want to help you, now Uncle's gone so suddenly."

"I'd like to believe that," she said slowly. Hesitantly she went on. "Mark, I don't want anything to change—at the iron works, I mean. Nobody will lose jobs. You can look forward to finishing at Cornell and after that, making the foundry your career. It was the way Richard wanted it. I want it that way, too. Will you tell the others?"

"You bet I will, Aunt Moira," he exclaimed boyishly, too naïve to hide his delighted relief. "To tell the truth, we were all a little worried."

"There's no need to be, no need at all."

A thin little man in blue serge lounge suit with a wing collar and polka dot bow tie was standing under an umbrella beside the funeral coach. As Moira Creegan approached

30

he gave a little bob with his head, tipping the brim of his black felt hat respectfully.

"Mister Davies would like you down at the office, Mrs. Creegan. For the will-reading. It's to be taken from the vault and opened before you all. Will you come? Good. I'll inform the others."

Moira stepped up into the coach and sank back gratefully against the upholstered seat. The past few days had been a real ordeal, sitting for hour after hour beside the casket, greeting all the friends of her dead husband, fighting the cold glances and resentful looks of the entire family. She had placed little Kathy with friends, thinking her too young to attend services. The family had objected to that, too.

No matter what she did or did not do, the 'family' always objected; not silently as it had while Richard was alive but with scarcely hidden sneers and rebuffs, or with words spoken just loud enough for her to overhear. She was too tired to fight them right now. In her own way she had loved Richard Ames Creegan and had made him a good wife. She regretted his dying quite sincerely.

The coach lurched as the horses began to move. Her head went back and forth on the seat cushion. Four days ago Mike Gannon had come to see Richard. She rather imagined he might still be in Rome. The consignment of iron ingots had been delayed by the period of mourning when the foundry and warehouses shut down. He had not come to the funeral services, though. Afraid that tongues might start to wag? A thin smile touched her mouth, bitter and resentful.

I wonder if I'll go back to seeing Mike, now that Richard's gone? Or will I let the family sway me—make me over into what it thinks Richard's widow should be? They might even try and arrange a match between cousin Jason and me—

Moira shuddered. Not Jason! She could not stand that. Perhaps she ought to take little Kathleen and go to Europe for a few months, give everyone a chance to forget, to dull the edge of their resentments. When they saw that by dying, Richard had not interfered with the even tenor of their lives, they might be better disposed toward her.

The matched bays were clop-clopping along Lynch Avenue, moving toward the center of town. The will-reading. Richard had told her often enough: she was to get every-

31

thing, the foundry, the warehouses, the farms in the hills, the stores along Main Street. She would be a very wealthy woman, she supposed. The old, old story of rags to riches. She would own a third of the city of Rome, just about. Hundreds of people would look to her for their livelihood.

Only five years ago she had been penniless.

She squirmed deeper into the coach upholstery, feeling warmth flood her veins. She ought not to feel such satisfaction, she supposed, but a body was human and it was the living who counted now, not the dead. There was little Kathleen to consider, too. She must be brought up properly, sent away to a fashionable girls' academy and then to a finishing school. The family would never look down its collective nose at the daughter the way it did at the mother.

The coach slowed beside the curb. The coachman sprang down to open her door. Moira inclined her head and smiled as she stepped out under the upraised umbrella. The coachman escorted her across the sidewalk. A law clerk was at the front door, holding it open.

Aunt Martha and the Tomkinses arrived almost on her heels. The young clerk walked ahead of them, opening a glass-paned door that entered a large room lined from floor to ceiling by bookshelves filled with legal tomes.

A long refectory table, its oak top polished almost to the brightness of a mirror, a dozen straight-backed chairs set about it, a thick maroon carpet and three standing ash trays, completed the furnishings of the library. Moira seated herself close to the tilt chair where Phineas Davies would read the will. There was a rustling of starched petticoats as Martha and Elvira joined her.

The clerk went into an adjoining office.

Moments later Phineas Davies came rushing in, carrying a manila portfolio wrapped with faded red ribbon and fastened by a large wax seal.

"This is our dear Richard's last will and testament, as you may have guessed," he said hurriedly, adjusting the ribboned pince-nez across the bridge of his nose. His fingers worked under the portfolio flap, breaking the wax seal. He drew it out and spread it flat with the palm of a hand as his eyes went around the room.

"This is not a new will," he said slowly. "Many times I warned Richard but he—hrummmph!" He cleared his throat, staring down at the neatly handwritten document.

"I shall read. I quote—"

" 'I, Richard Ames Creegan, residing now in Rome, Oneida County, New York, do hereby revoke all wills and codicils, as well as all other instruments of a testamentary nature heretofore made by me, and do hereby make, publish and declare this to be my last will and testament, in manner and form following:

" 'First: I give, devise and bequeath all of my stock in Creegan Iron Works Corporation, together with such bonds as may or may not also appear in my name, to my sister Martha Creegan and to my sister Elvira Tomkins, in equal and joint ownership . . .' "

Moira heard a triumphant gasp from Aunt Martha.

A sibilant voice whispered, "It's all right, I tell you. We're safe—safe! She doesn't get a penny!"

Moira paid little or no attention to the interruptions. Instead, she sat in a daze, staring at the bald lawyer and his pince-nez which bobbled crazily at almost every word.

" ' . . . give, devise and bequeath to my nephew Jason Evans Tomkins the sum of ten thousand dollars to be . . .' "

Oh, no—no!

" ' . . . in witness hereof I have on this fifteenth day of June, 1878, signed, sealed, published and declared this to be my last will and—' "

Moira sat up straight, understanding coming to her in a flood of sickness. The will was dated June, 1878—two full years before their marriage! Even before Richard had met her! *Oh, my God!* Why, that meant she did not share in the estate! She got nothing—not a penny—neither she nor little Kathleen.

They were paupers!

The room was silent as Phineas Davies, without lifting his eyes, said, "Richard always intended to make a new will, Mrs. Creegan. He just never got around to it. He was a busy man. I warned him often enough that he might be jeopardizing your interests, as well as those of your daughter, Kathleen. He always agreed. He told me it was his intention to make a new will, leaving everything to you."

The lawyer shrugged his narrow shoulders. "There will come a day when a man will not be permitted, either by oversight as is the case here, or by willful and deliberate intent, to disinherit his wife. Unfortunately, that day is not yet here."

Aunt Martha was standing. "Phineas Davies, there is no need to apologize to Mrs. Creegan. I'm sure you mean well, ᵕ but spare your concern. Little Kathleen will be well cared for, I assure you. After all, she *is* Richard's daughter."

Moira gasped and whirled, crying out. "Kathleen? You wouldn't dare! Kathleen is mine. I'm her mother."

Aunt Elvira hissed, "A fine mother you are! No court in the land would let you keep her!"

"How dare you! Richard said you were vicious but—"

Moira came to her feet, eyes staring down at the bitter features of the woman, at the troubled, uneasy faces of the men. Phineas Davies lifted his hands, saying, "Please ladies!"

Elvira snapped, "Richard left his holdings to Martha and me. That means you're our lawyer, Phineas. I want you to prepare legal proceedings so that Martha and I may adopt Kathleen immediately."

Aunt Martha sniffed and nodded, smiling coldly. To one side, Frederick Tomkins pursed his lips thoughtfully, toying with the heavy gold watch chain that crossed his vested belly. Mark stared down at his hands. Jason was looking up at the ceiling, head back and stretched out comfortably in his armchair, lips curved in a triumphant grin.

The lawyer said gently, "May I point out that you could take Kathleen away from Mrs. Creegan only if she were an unfit mother, or unable to support the child?"

"She's both!" snapped Aunt Martha.

"I have the house on Depeyster Street and my jewels," exclaimed Moira. "And—and I'll find employment of some sort."

"Not in Rome, you won't," said Elvira, folding her hands in her lap. "Phineas, I want you to draw up papers to prevent this woman from taking Kathleen—whatever they call it—"

"A writ of injunction," murmured her husband.

"Thank you, Frederick. A writ of injunction to prevent Mrs. Creegan from taking the child out of Rome. This very afternoon. I want her served with these papers by sundown. That way she won't be able to run off behind our backs. Jason!"

Jason leaped upright. "Yes, Mother?"

"Get a constable and take him out to your poor, dear departed Uncle Richard's house on Depeyster Street—which now belongs to all of us—and station him there to prevent Mrs. Creegan from entering and taking any of our property."

"Right away, Mother!"

34

Moira felt her legs weakening under her. A flood of tears seemed poised to burst from her eyelids, but she'd be damned if she'd give these vultures the satisfaction! Adventuress, was she? And fortune hunter? Her right hand balled into a fist.

"You won't get away with it," she cried fiercely. "I'll fight you through every court in the land!"

"Court fights cost money," sniffed Aunt Martha. "According to what I heard just now, you don't have a blessed penny to your name."

"I'll find the money somewhere."

Aunt Elvira smiled coldly. "By selling yourself to some other deluded man, Mrs. Creegan? I've no doubt you could do that. But would he want Richard's child? It's a point to consider."

Her hands came up to her cheeks as Moira reeled. This was a fantastic nightmare. Oh, she'd known they'd never liked her, this family, but to find them so vindictive, so filled with hate and resentment! The tears were coming. She could fight them no longer.

Even as the sob burst in her throat, she stumbled around the edge of the table and ran for the hall door. There was no law clerk to open it for her now that she was penniless. Her gloved hand fumbled for the knob, turning it. The tears were stinging her eyes, blinding her.

The door opened. She was in the hall and running . . .

CHAPTER THREE

Captain Mike Gannon was flipping a hawser rope from the piling on the basin dock when he heard the rattle of coach wheels. He paid no attention to them. He was overdue now on his run from Rome to Buffalo. Four days he had been held up while the town buried Richard Ames Creegan. Lost days cost him money, and he was in a sour mood. The basin dock was empty, save for himself and his driver. Everyone was gone, this hour after quitting time.

The last rope thumped across the dock planks.

He stepped onto the deck of the big barge. The gossip in the bars along Basin Street told him plainly enough there was no love lost between the family and the widowed Mrs. Creegan. Mike was the only friend she had, but she had ignored him. She hadn't sent for him, now that she was a rich widow.

"Guess I'm not good enough for her any more—her and her fancy ways and house," he grumbled, moving along the deck to the forward cabin. Beneath his feet the barge appeared to sway a little in the water. "Time was, Moira Kennally liked to talk to me."

His hand was on the cabin door when a voice screamed at him. "Mike—oh, Mike! Wait for me!"

He whirled, seeing Moira Creegan in a black dress and black velvet hat running across the loading area, a bundle in her arms. With a vague uneasiness he turned away from the cabin.

"Faith, you needn't run so fast to say good-bye," he grinned, his good nature restored. "All you had to do was send word."

He became aware of her white face and the tears streaking her cheeks. He sprang forward, his hands going out to catch her by a wrist. He swung her across the water between the dock timbers and the deck of the canal barge.

"Sure you've gone and worked yourself up into a fine fit of crying, haven't you?" And then, because he could not forget the agony of the long years without her, he added, "And what's a swell lady like yourself got to cry about? You're a rich woman—"

"Mike, will you shut up!"

He goggled, seeing the anger flare in her face.

She beat his chest with a fist. "Get me out of sight, you Irish lunkhead. If anybody sees me with you, it'll be too bad for both of us."

He saw that the bundle she held was little Kathy, sleeping soundly. Something told him not to ask questions. His huge hand caught her elbow, steered her along the deck and to a low bench along the tiller-rail.

"Sit there. If there's so much need for hurry, let me get the *Lucky Penny* out into the canal. Nobody will notice you here."

His arm made a sweeping motion to his driver who sent a ripple along his reins as his voice urged the mules against the traces. The towlines shook and lengthened, grew taut. As the hooves dug deeper into the dirt towpath, the barge

36

slid forward through the water. Mike put a hand on the tiller, holding it steady.

Behind him Moira Creegan wept silently, head bowed.

For a full thirty minutes Mike let the *Lucky Penny* surge through the canal waters, putting distance between the Rome basin and his barge. Twilight lay in a darkening hush across the land. It was time to stop and anchor for the night but he kept putting it off, wanting to let the miles grow in his wake. Until he could see no more, he stood at his tiller. Then he called to his driver and swung his whip-staff over, the huge rudder creaking as it responded.

Moira looked up at him. "Why are we stopping, Mike? Keep going, please. If you don't, they'll catch up to us and take Kathy away from me."

"It's night, Moira. You know canal travel as well as I do. When the sun sets, travel stops."

"Couldn't we make an exception?"

"And run full tilt into some other barge? I kept going a full ten minutes longer'n I should have. Maybe you'd better tell me what this is all about. You look like you've lost your last friend."

She smiled bitterly, lips quirking downward. "I have— all except you. Richard forgot to make a new will when we married. It's that simple. Everything he had goes to his dear, dear sisters and their families. Until this afternoon I was a wealthy widow. Now I'm nothing. The Tomkinses have a police constable at the Depeyster Street house to see I take nothing away with me. . . ."

The story came out in a harsh, hollow voice as she sat rocking back and forth, arms clasping her sleeping child. Mike listened incredulously in the darkness, not stirring, not speaking until her words ran out and she sat silent and unseeing, huddled up in a knot.

"Jesus, girl. No wonder you ran like the devil was at your heels. They want your baby, do they? Well, now. Maybe we can do something about that. Marry me and to hell with the Creegans and the Martins."

Her smile was tender as she reached for his hand. "I ought to marry you, Mike. It's what you've always wanted. But I have no heart for marriage right now. The thought of it gags me after what I went through with my precious in-laws in Phineas Davies' office."

He frowned at the hand clinging to his own. "So you

37

won't marry me," he growled. "All right, stand on your own feet for a while. I can wait a little longer."

Her head was tilted as she stared up at him. "Go on, Mike. Ask it. How am I going to support my baby? It's what you're thinking, isn't it?"

His cheeks flushed in the darkness. "Sure, I'm a damned fool to be so obvious. You've no need to support yourself while I can move an arm and a leg. You're welcome to what I have—"

"Mike, Mike," she whispered fiercely. "You still don't understand. I want independence! I want to be free of the need to depend on a man for support. Those few minutes with Martha and Elvira taught me a bitter lesson. I want to earn the money I need. I *will* earn it."

"How?" he asked bluntly.

"I don't know. All I can do, I suppose, is sing and play a piano."

"You do that well enough," he admitted. "But you know what the world thinks of a public entertainer."

"A harlot, you mean to say. The world thinks her a whore. Is that it, Mike?" She lifted her face and even in the darkness—there was a faint moon lifting into the sky—he could see her eyes flash.

"I guess that's what I mean," he muttered.

"Oh, don't be shy with me. I'm a married woman now and not the virgin girl you kissed five years ago. I know the way a man is made and the things that please a man."

"Christ, woman! Will you be still!"

Her smile was gentle, almost tender. "Why should I be still, Michael Gannon? Do I shock you, speaking this way? Aunt Elvira and Aunt Martha as good as called me a harlot this afternoon. That's just a polite way of saying I laid Richard into his marriage bed, isn't it?"

"Moira, you're only torturing yourself."

"It's time we looked at the world the way it is and not the way we'd like it to be. You wanted to marry me five years ago. I picked Richard Creegan because he was rich. I went to him a virgin, despite what his sisters think and say. Now I'm his widow and penniless. I'm on your barge and on my way to Buffalo to find employment. I don't even have enough money to pay my fare."

"Jesus, woman! Damned if I'll listen to—"

"Mike, you've got to listen. If you've ever loved me—if you love me now—you'll let me talk. I want you to under-

38

stand me, Mike. I don't care about the rest of the world but I want you to know.

"I'll stand on my own two feet. I insist upon it. Never again will I be beholden to any man, not even to you. Never again will I find myself in the position I'm in now, because of a man. Richard forgot to make a will though he had five years in which to do it, and so I have to run away like a common thief with my own child. Can you understand a little of what I feel right now, Mike?"

"Och," he said furiously and stared out over the rail.

She did not move for a long time. Then there was the rustle of a taffeta underskirt and she was at his elbow, so close that he could smell her perfume and know the touch of her flesh against his arm.

"Do you have a place where Kathy can sleep, Mike? And a galley? I'll cook your food for you as part payment for my fare."

Mike Gannon turned slowly. His face was hard and grim in the moonlight. "You know I'd never take payment from you, Moira Creegan, for any service you let me do for you."

Her smile was bright. "Then it's off the barge you'll be putting us? Like skulking thieves caught stealing a penny sweet?"

He had to laugh at her rich brogue. "All right. Come forward with me. Abe—my driver—will have brought the mules on board and tied us up by now. Come forward to the cabin with me. I'll show you where you can put the little one, and the galley where we store our food."

Within minutes the galley was alight with two brass wall lamps. Moira stood at the tin-lined wooden sink, peeling half a dozen potatoes, with her black bombazine sleeves rolled up to her elbows and a torn cloth belted at her waist to serve as apron. Kathleen was sleeping in an improvised bed near the west wall of the main cabin. Mike stood in the companionway, his eyes eating her alive.

"We're almost like married folks," he said at last, heavily and with wistfulness in his voice.

"What about your driver? Will he eat with us?"

"Not old Abe. He'd be too embarrassed. He'd a lot sooner eat with the mules than with a woman. No offense intended, of course."

Moira laughed richly. Watching her, Mike thought glumly that if she were his wife he'd have the right to bed her whenever he felt like it. His stare slid over her round hips pressing into the black bombazine and up her side to the firm bulge made by a full, ripe breast as her fingers peeled potatoes. The way she shook under the black stuff of her dress made his mouth go dry.

"I've a bottle of Irish whiskey stashed away somewhere in here," he muttered. "Would you be caring for a short one?"

Her wrist pushed back a fallen lock of thick black hair, as her blue eyes danced in amusement. "I would, Michael Gannon. Very much."

They drank the fiery liquor and began eating the bacon and eggs and potatoes Moira had hash-browned in the big iron skillet. It was warm in the tiny galley with the stove so close to their table, and soon Moira was undoing the buttons of her standing collar, opening the dress down to the deep cleft of her bosom. Mike tried not to stare. They would be several days together on the barge. He might as well understand now there was a *hands off* sign on Moira Creegan. She was no Canal Street trull to tumble into his bunk with him when he crooked a finger.

He sighed heavily and went on eating.

Dawn found the *Lucky Penny* moving steadily through the canal waters past Syracuse and on into Finger Lakes country, through neat farmlands where red barns and grazing cows added a pastoral dignity to long rolling green hills and apple orchards. Stone fences divided the meadows into neat geometrical patterns. Occasionally a group of boys with fishing poles across their shoulders waved straw hats.

Moira sat on the cabin roof braiding her black hair, comfortable in camisole and bare feet, with little Kathy playing with a toy boat Mike had whittled out of a broken capstan bar. She was a strangely contented woman this morning. Rome and the Creegan family lay far behind as the barge pushed its way toward Buffalo at a steady four knots an hour.

From time to time she glanced shyly at Mike. He had been so happy with her last night, eating the food she cooked and helping with the dishes. There'd been something boyish about big Mike Gannon with his whistling and his jokes and the yearning to take her in his arms deep in his eyes.

She ought not to be mooning about Mike Gannon but

40

worrying about her future in Buffalo. She had to make a living for herself and Kathy. It might not be too easy. Mike had hinted as much last night as they stood on the deck leaning against the rail, staring up at the moon.

"Things aren't too good these days," he'd said. "Money's tight, but you don't need to worry about money. I have plenty."

"I won't take your money, Mike. I want you to understand that."

"You always were a proud woman," he growled

"Too proud at least to take money from a man when I have no way of paying it back."

She smiled as she stretched out on the cabin roof, closing her eyes, letting the warm sun beat on her. Yesterday seemed like a nightmare, soon to be forgotten. The future was all that mattered, her future with little Kathy. She squirmed into a more comfortable position. Soon she fell asleep.

When she woke she found it had grown chilly and that Mike had covered her with his greatcoat. Her glance went to Kathy who was sitting on the rail bench near Mike, solemnly eating a slice of bread thickly larded with butter. Mike himself seemed scarcely to have moved, still standing with the tiller in his hands, staring forward.

Snuggling deeper into the greatcoat, she drew it about her and rose to a sitting position on the cabin roof.

"Don't you ever get tired of just standing there?" she asked.

Her question drew his eyes to her. He shook his head, smiling faintly. "I'm used to it. And there are worse ways to make a living."

"If the Creegans learn it was you who got me out of Rome you may lose your account with them."

"It would be a small loss, believe me."

"I don't want to cause you trouble, Mike."

"What trouble can the Creegans cause? Just put them out of your mind."

She slipped off the cabin roof and came to stand beside him. "Show me how to steer the barge, Mike. I can spell you for a little while."

He showed her the huge wooden whipstaff and the manner of its handling. In her bare feet she was much smaller than the canal man. His nearness made her heart pound, she discovered. She was forced to concentrate on what he said

41

in order to overcome the sensual pleasure she felt as his arm went about her shoulders and his hands fell on her fingers where they held the steering pole.

After she discovered the knack of it, she began to enjoy the sensation of playing helmsman. Her laughter rang out when she found she could control the barge with a simple motion of her arm. After a while Mike came out of the galley with hot coffee and sandwiches.

The day went quickly. There were so many things to see at the rail—a whole new world was opening up to her.

That night she and Kathy slept more soundly than they'd slept in a long time. The sun and the wind and all that fresh air weighted her eyelids until she almost dozed over the evening meal. Mike shooed them off to bed, assuring her he would clean up, that he was used to doing it.

For once she did not argue.

Two days later they were moving past Lockport, on the last leg of the trip. Tomorrow morning a little before noon they would be docking along Canal Street in Buffalo. There was a sadness in Mike Gannon as he went about roping the *Lucky Penny* to a canal piling.

The past few days had been among the happiest in his life, though he felt a twinge of guilt because he held the barge almost to a crawl so as to prolong the hours. If it were up to him, the trip would never end.

"One last night," he muttered. After tonight Moira Creegan would go her own way. She would start a new life in which there would be no place for Mike Gannon. She might meet a man, somebody who'd catch her fancy more than he did. She might even marry him.

He groaned. There had been a number of moments when he'd thought he'd go mad if he couldn't take her in his arms and cover her mouth with kisses. The first night they'd spent on the barge, for instance, when he'd gone into the cabin to make sure Kathy was covered and the moonlight had been so bright he could not help but glance at Moira with the covers up to her middle and only the thin lawn of her corset cover veiling her firm breasts. God! How he had wanted her!

The way she walked about in the camisole with her hips shifting enticingly at every stride maddened him. Just to be near her was all he asked, though as a man he admitted

42

he wanted more of her than just her company. An insatiable hunger was in him for the touch of her hand on his as they stood together at the tiller or for the sound of her laughter ringing out at something he'd said. He lived for the quiet serenity of the nights after Kathy had been put to sleep and they stood side by side at the barge rail listening to the gurgling waters and watching the lights in neighboring farms go off one by one as the world fell asleep around them.

She felt the way he did, he was sure. A tenderness smiled out at him from her eyes at times, and she took the opportunity of brushing against him occasionally as if to reassure herself that this was no dream she lived. Twice he'd caught her in his arms to tell her how much she meant to him and to beg her to marry him, but each time she'd slipped away with low laughter bubbling in her throat.

As he moved toward the barge galley, he paused to stare through the porthole, eyes drinking in the sight of Moira moving back and forth from stove to counter. She had only the one change of clothes, the black bombazine dress, so she was forced to make do with camisole and corset cover. Right now she wore the thin sleeveless camisole, together with a flounced petticoat. For ease of movement she'd left off her corset, and the linen clung to the rounded contours of her hips and traced the outline of firm thighs as she moved.

Gannon felt his throat go dry.

He wanted this woman so badly he was forced to stroll twice about the deck so that his pounding blood might quiet, so that he could walk into the galley and smile at her without reaching out and pulling her into his arms. She glanced at him out of the corners of her eyes, smiling faintly.

"You were a long time tonight, Mike."

"There was work to be done," he muttered.

"I thought I saw you at the porthole a little while ago. I must have been mistaken."

"I glanced in," he said casually, moving to the wash basin, filling it with tepid water.

As he washed he grew aware that she stood by with a clean towel. She was too close to him in that white camisole through which he could see the enticing circles of her dark nipples.

She held out the towel but his hands went past the coarse

cotton to slide up bare arms to her shoulders. "Mike," she whispered, not drawing back, just pleading with her eyes.

"Yes," he said heavily, letting his fingers bunch in the towel. "Yes, of course." But he had the feeling that they were only putting off for a little while this need which lay between them.

He ate slowly, eyes intent on the woman who sat across from him, who reached out to her child from time to time, making sure she finished her vegetables, buttering bread for her, seemingly unaware of the big man who kept them company.

Mike started the dishes while Moira was putting little Kathy to bed. His every sense was alert to the sounds coming from the other room, the quick steps Moira made from the wash stand to the sawed-off crate which served Kathleen as a bunk, the muffled laughter of the little girl and the low murmured prayer she said.

Then Moira was beside him suddenly. He had not heard her come from the inner room. The brush of her hip against his thigh and the warmth of her arm sent a flood of fire through his veins. One hand went to her hip, stroking the smooth flesh through the linen camisole and drawing her back against him.

"Mike, I—"

His mouth smothered her words, even as his arm circled her middle, holding her firmly. His hand turned her so that he could feel the softness of her belly pressing against him. He forced her back against the lead-lined wooden sink, letting her know the solid strength of his body.

For an instant she was limp and boneless. Then a moan formed deep in her throat as she brought her bare arms up and locked them about his neck. She opened her mouth wide and her tongue lashed outward between his lips as she came into his arms.

"You want me, don't you, Mike? Ah, you don't have to answer. I can tell well enough. God forgive me, I want you, too."

She tried to fight the molten longing that filled her thighs and belly. She was Moira Kennally Creegan, not a trull off Canal Street. Though she knew Mike Gannon loved her and she loved him, this terrible throbbing in her body was like nothing she had ever known before. Unable to control her own responses, she found herself moving back

44

and forth against him, crooning softly deep in her throat.

"Mike, oh Mike! What are you doing to me with your kisses and your hands? I'm a married woman but I've never felt anything like this craziness—"

Her hands were on his shirt, ripping it, and then her teeth were nibbling at the flesh of his chest. Only vaguely was she aware of his startled cry, of his delighted surprise. Her fingernails were buried in his arms and she moved steadily and urgently, linking her soft loins hotly and wantonly to him.

Her breasts were swollen, startling white in the lamplight as his fingers drew her camisole downward. When his lips touched them, she cried out harshly. Then his arms were lifting her, carrying her across•the galley and into the bunkroom. The petticoat and camisole came away as he tumbled her onto the neatly made bunk. She still wore her black silk stockings and high-buttoned shoes but above them she was naked.

"Hurry, Mike—darling!" she panted.

His great hands ripped off his sweater and threw it aside. In a moment he towered huge and muscular above her. Seeing him so powerful and so ready, her eyes widened. Sobbing uncontrollably, she writhed across the quilt, pulling him down to her.

Their love-making was not the tender mating it might have been five years ago but a desperate search for pleasure, an attempt to make up in this frenzied instant for all their lost yesterdays. Her agile hips drove savagely in a steadily increasing tempo and her ecstatic cries were muffled by the shoulder against which she pressed her mouth.

During the night he drew her to him many times. Always she came willingly, eager to be used, letting his hands and his lips take their will of her, building an urgent need in her flesh over and over again. She twisted against him, her hands fondling and caressing his hard masculine flesh until he groaned with delight.

"Five years, Mike. We've got to make up for five wasted years! I've been a fool, darling. Make me know how much of a fool I've been. Make me, make me!"

They fell asleep in a warm tangled heap of arms and legs.

CHAPTER FOUR

Ten days later, Moira Creegan was looking for a job.

She had been to one theater after another in Buffalo, to saloons and restaurants. There was no work for a pianist or a singer. Even the men whose eyes lighted up at sight of her attractiveness shook their heads. The entertainment business was moving at a slow pace. Come back three months from now, they told her.

Three months! At the mere thought of it, her stomach turned over inside her. She could starve to death in three months. She would already have starved if Mike Gannon had not insisted she take a hundred dollars from him as a loan.

The money had enabled her to put little Kathy in Jennings House, a boarding house run by a childless couple who assured her that they would dearly enjoy taking care of the little girl. Moira had passed herself off as a businesswoman whose affairs took her great distances at times, even as far west as Cleveland and Chicago. Her husband was dead and she had no family with whom to leave her daughter, she informed them.

"Let us take care of her, Mrs. Creegan," plump Mrs. Jennings had gushed, lifting Kathy in her arms and squeezing her. "It'll be almost as if she belonged to Tom and me."

Jealousy stabbed into Moira when she saw how Kathy was hugging the woman but she told herself that it was only for a little while, just until she could get on her feet. Now as she moved across Lafayette Square and up Clinton Street toward a German beer garden, she was beginning to wonder if she would ever achieve financial independence.

Mike was back on the canal, piloting the *Lucky Penny* to Albany and would not return for another week. She had two crumpled dollar bills in her purse and the rent would be due again, day after tomorrow.

A heavy-set German was standing at the entrance to the *Biergarten.* He moved the crook-handled pipe from his

46

mouth as she stopped in front of him and considered her with pale blue eyes.

"*Nein*, no job." he muttered at last, shaking his head dolefully. "Not iff you vas Jenny Lind vould I haff a job for you. Times is badt."

He spat and looked down at his pipe. "Maybe you could gedt a job on Canal Street. They use a lodt of singers there."

"Oh," Moira said, suddenly remembering that Mike had said something about Canal Street on the long trip from Rome. "Thank you. Thank you very much."

She turned on a worn heel and walked south along Clinton Street. What was it Mike had said? A sin street, yes; she remembered that much of course. But he'd said a name, a coffin or—"The Mummy Case!" she breathed.

Canal Street lay south of The Terrace, which was a wide city square between Court and Genesee Streets. A man could find just about whatever vice he craved, if he was willing to pay for it.

The good fathers of Buffalo hated Canal Street, and from time to time attempts were made to clean it up. The police Black Maria would clang along its cobblestoned length and prostitutes and known criminals were caught by the scruffs of their necks—not without a lot of bitter fighting, she guessed—and tossed into the barred wagon. For a few days the street would be quiet, then it would flare up again.

"Sure, it's a blight on the face of the city," Mike Gannon had told her. "The rest of Buffalo wants it wiped out or cleaned up. But nothing every gets done. It's as if Canal Street were a kind of sickness that takes time and rest to to cure. New York City has its Bowery, San Francisco its Barbary Coast, London its Whitechapel. Why can't Buffalo have Canal Street?"

Why not, indeed? thought Moira Creegan as she angled her stride to the south. Her chin was lifted defiantly though her heart was thudding with excitement. If it gave her a job and a livelihood, she'd be grateful.

As she came off The Terrace the houses around her began to change. The buildings were old and worn, with the bare wood showing where paint had been flayed away by wind and rain. In some houses the windows gaped paneless, in others the glass was cracked or broken. She might have

47

thought them tenantless except that from time to time she glimpsed a movement of sorts, as if someone had heard her footsteps approaching and had run to catch a look at her.

The further she went, the worse the houses became.

Once she almost turned back, for she could see drunken men now, some leaning against the walls of dilapidated buildings, others lying in the gutter where slops and garbage had been spilled.

Moira remembered the fine words she had spoken to Mike Gannon. "I'm going to stand on my own two feet. Never again will I be beholden to any man."

She saw the brightly painted sign that was carved to represent a mummy case from three blocks away. Long since she had become aware of the fact that she was the only female on the street, and that as bleary eyes focused on her attractiveness they recognized her for an interloper, a stranger.

Two or three times drunken men had accosted her, but the loathing on her face was so plain to read that they had not spoken in invitation but only with obscene vituperation.

At the head of an alleyway three men were fighting viciously, with fists and teeth and boots. One man was down, bleeding from the mouth, his body moving inertly as the others kicked in his ribs. It had been hard to repress a scream at that moment, so great had been her horror and her fright. She had kept quiet only because of an inner certainty that if she attracted attention to herself she would be dragged into a dark alleyway and raped.

She saw women, too, blowzy creatures with unkempt hair and with only torn rags to cover their nakedness, peering from open windows or standing in wrappers and kimonos at the doors of the little sheds that served them as homes.

Then the wooden sign was creaking overhead on rusty chains and her buttoned shoes were moving up the porch steps. The glass-panelled door opened easily to her hand.

The interior of The Mummy Case was dim and quiet in this early afternoon. Moira studied the long bar, the sawdust floor, the brass spittoons. Her gaze flicked across the huge oil painting of a voluptuous woman stretched out invitingly on cushions above and behind the bar.

"Anybody here?" she called.

There was no answer. A little more boldly, she stepped into the sawdust and let the door swing shut behind her.

"Hello up there," she shouted. "Anybody around?"

48

"Who's that?" somebody called from the second floor. "Cora? Maybelle? Margot?"

She heard footsteps sound on the hallway runner, muffled and indistinct. A woman came to the head of the stairs and stared down.

"Who the hell are you?" asked The Egyptian.

"My—my name is Moira Creegan. Mi—Mike Gannon sent me."

The dusky woman put a hand to her tousled brown hair, pushing it around as if its weight bothered her thinking. "Captain Gannon of the *Lucky Line?*" she asked. "Now why in hell would he send a woman like you down into this hell-hole?"

Moira smiled faintly. "To get a job."

"A *job?*"

"I'm a widow. I can play the piano and sing a little. I'm desperate. I've tramped all over the city seeking work. I need money."

For the space of ten heartbeats The Egyptian looked at her. Then she made a little gesture with a hand. "Come on up, dearie. Let's you and me talk." She stood to one side as Moira came up the stairs, but her eyes were brightly alert, studying her from the tips of her shoes to the top of her pert Langtry bonnet.

As Moira came level with her, the darker woman drew her wrapper together at her throat. They were of a height, she saw, and would make the same sensual appeal to men. From the way her dress rode across her hips and waist, and mounded so firmly at her bosom, her body appeared ripe and full. Put this woman in a pair of tights and black mesh hose—

"Let's go look over the merchandise, honey," she muttered. As they moved along the hall carpet, she glanced sideways at her companion. "You got any objection to wearing some kind of costume, something tight and reveal-ing?"

"You mean to show off my—my body for men to look at? Oh, I couldn't do that. I really couldn't."

The other woman shrugged. "You could play a piano like Tchaikovsky and sing like Kate Vaughn and it wouldn't mean a thing. Men don't come here for culture. They want to see a woman, what she looks like, maybe dream a little about her."

"I'm sorry," Moira exclaimed helplessly. "I just couldn't."

49

The Egyptian regarded her a long moment. "All right. It's up to you. No skin off my nose. Give my best to Mike when you see him."

"Isn't there anything else? A waitress? Maybe a hat-check girl?"

"I use tough waiters, in case a fight breaks out, as it does two, three nights a week—"

Moira felt panic rise inside her as she turned to leave. The Mummy Case had been her last hope. Now it was gone. The sound of her footfalls going down the carpeted staircase tapped out a funeral dirge in her heart.

She stood on Canal Street in front of The Mummy Case and felt sickness build into nausea inside her. Never had she felt so much alone. Hands clasped tight to her purse, she began walking in the direction from which she had come.

A gray rat ran across the street ahead of her. She put a hand to her mouth to stifle a scream. From a window overhead a woman leaned down, cackling laughter. "Give you a start, did it dearie? Can't say as I blame you. Never did cotton to them rats."

Shuddering, Moira went on. Dusk was throwing long shadows across the houses and lamplights were being turned on here and there. In the corners of dark alleyways men were standing, slouching. Realization came to her suddenly that she was the only woman in sight.

Fear came crawling down her spine an instant later. Her sidewise glances let her know these were human derelicts, with torn and mended garments, reeking of whiskey and urine. God! If one of them reached for her, to drag her screaming into the mouth of a forbiddingly dark alley and throw up her skirt—

A whimper began, deep in her throat. "God above, let me get out of this place unharmed."

"Hold up there, honey," a voice called.

She cast a glance over a shoulder, seeing an unwashed face and blackened teeth showing where thick lips were drawn back in a ratlike grin. The man put out a hand, half running. The fingers caught her shoulder, yanked her backward.

"No harm meant, lady," the black-toothed man chuckled, his eyes roving. "I got half a dollar to spend. Easy money for you, if you want some cash."

She tried to cry out but the muscles of her throat seemed paralyzed. The tramp took her silence for assent. "Sure, you

50

want some money. Me and the boys, we'll see you get a few bucks for being nice to us."

Her glance went beyond him toward the half dozen men waiting in the alley shadows. The hand was drawing her along helplessly. Only when one of the waiting men began to fumble at his trousers did she break free of that agonized paralysis. She screamed, head back and mouth open.

The others cursed and ran forward. A dirty hand went over her lips, stifling her outcry. In that moment of insane terror, she heard the shrill note of a police whistle. She fought savagely now, feet braced against the cobblestones, wrenching away from the hands that mauled her.

Heavy brogans came pounding through the twilight. She saw a nightstick swing, heard the dull thud as it connected with a head. Then the broad bulks of three policemen were beside her, clubs flailing until they were bloody.

In a few seconds she was free of pawing hands, watching one man beaten to his knees with his face all bloody while others dropped to lie motionless in a puddle of slops. One of the policemen turned and came for her.

"You there! Don't you know better than to go selling yourself on the street like this?"

Indignation made her flush. "Selling myself? I'll have you know I was visiting The Mummy Case—"

A cop winked. "One of The 'Gyptian's gals, hey? You're a new one. We haven't see you around before."

Almost of their own volition, Moira felt her shoulders lift into a shrug. What did it matter? What did anything matter any more? She was hungry. Kathy was hungry. The only way she could get food was to pay for it. To pay for it meant she had to have money. To get money, she needed a job. Any sort of job. Even one where she wore something that would show off her body to any man who wanted to look at her.

Two policemen offered their arms. "We'll escort you back to The Mummy Case, ma'am. So nobody else bothers you. What kind of an act do you do?"

"Act? I don't know. I haven't thought about it yet."

A thick laugh cut into her despair. "Whatever it is, I'm coming to see it."

She moved like an automaton between the bluecoated officers along the cobbles, up the porch steps and in through the glass doors of The Mummy Case. The woman who called

51

herself The Egyptian was at the bar, talking to a bartender lighting an overhead lamp. She swung around, staring.

"We brought one of your girls back, Lily."

"I changed my mind," Moira said weakly.

The Egyptian smiled and waved a hand at the bar. "Come in, boys. Joe, set up my friends to whiskey and beer. You come along with me, honey. I know just the sort of job you'd be good at."

Two nights later, Moira Creegan sat huddled on the bench of a small dressing table in a tiny room a few feet from The Mummy Case stage. She was biting her lower lip hard to stop her tears from ruining her mascaraed eyes and rouged cheeks. She could not do it! It was unthinkable. To go out on that stage and take off her clothes—every last stitch—would mark her for nothing more than a fallen woman!

Oh, my God! Mike, where are you? If you were here now I'd throw myself at you! I'd marry you in a minute.

"A steak, honey," The Egyptian had promised. "After you do your act. There isn't anything to it, really. You pretend you're in your bedroom, see? You shuck out of everything and let the boys get a look at you. Then you slip a nightie over your head and blow out the candle."

A fist rapped her door. "Five minutes, five minutes."

Moira's legs felt numb as she stood up. She wanted to scream and run, but there was no place to go, nobody to care whether she screamed or not. For a fleeting instant she thought of Aunt Elvira Tomkins and Aunt Martha Creegan. Her hand went to the doorknob. It turned easily in her hand.

The Egyptian was in the wings, gesturing. "They've set up the bed and the night table. There—Johnny's lighting the candle. Go out as soon as the curtain starts to lift. You understand?"

Moira nodded dumbly.

Then the curtain was rising and she was striding forward, stretching and yawning as The Egyptian had taught her, trying not to look out over the long room but unable to resist the sudden glance. She whispered a prayer for thankfulness that the lamps had been turned down low. At least she could not see the men in the audience clearly.

Her fingers had been working at the cloth buttons of her Polonaise gown. She threw back the flaps and began to slide the jacket down her bare arms. A black corselet gripped her breasts, she leaned forward to slide down the gown, she realized with a hot wave of shame that she was exposing them entirely. The room was very still. She could hear the hard breathing of the staring men.

Her hand tossed the dress over a chair. Again she stretched and yawned, arms high over her head. She was a woman going to bed, no more. *If these men were so taken by her exhibition, let them look. Let them look all they wanted.*

She told herself this but there were tears in her eyes as she bent to unfasten the garters which held up her black stockings. In the candlelight no one would see her tears, however. Maybe because nobody was looking at her face. The orchestra struck up the tune of *Frankie and Johnny*.

Moira's fingers rolled down a wispy stocking of ebony silk and lifted it off her white feet. The stocking trailed through the air as she tossed it after the gown. She began to sing softly, but no one paid any attention. Every sense was focused on the length of one shapely white leg, visible from toes to hip as the men waited for the other leg to be revealed. She bent to roll down the other stocking.

Turning, she unhooked her corselet, revealing a bare white back. The corselet went away and now she stood naked in the candlelight.

She was supposed to swing around, to let them see all of her. She could not. No matter if The Egyptian paid her nothing, she just could not do it. With trembling hands she reached for the nightgown, lifted it over her head and let it drift down about her hips and thighs. Bending, she blew out the candle.

Sobbing freely, she ran from the stage, not hearing the shrill whistles and the pounding of hands, the stomping of heavy feet. She wept for half an hour before the knuckles tapped on her dressing room door. The knob turned and The Egyptian entered.

"You should have taken a couple of bows. They liked you. But you didn't like them, did you?"

"They're animals!"

"Well, what else? But they use the same kind of money we do, honey. Don't ever forget that." She continued to stare at Moira, her eyes soft and full of a rare kind of understanding, then shook her head. "You just aren't cut out for this sort of thing. A shame, really. We might have made quite a success of our stage show with you around."

"I'm sorry," Moira whispered.

The Egyptian laughed. "Hell, forget it. Come on out and eat your steak. You've earned yourself twenty bucks, anyhow. That's better than nothing."

"You won't want me after—after tonight, will you?"

"Sure, I want you. But what about you? Can you go through with it again tomorrow night, and the night after that and—?"

"No!" Moira screamed, clenching her fists and drumming them on the dressing-table top. "No, no, no!"

All next day, The Egyptian was at her with words.

"It isn't so hard, honey, just taking off your clothes on a stage. Hell, you can't beat the hours. And the pay isn't so bad, either."

"I can't do it again. I just can't." A cold misery worked inside Moira and her lovely face was ragged with worry.

"Of course not, if you say so. But I heard a lot of applause last night. If I know anything about men—and I do —we'll have an overflow crowd tonight. Now, just suppose I up the ante to thirty dollars? Thirty dollars will buy your little girl a lot of milk and cookies."

"Please," Moira whispered hoarsely.

Yet she stayed at The Mummy Case all day long, too ashamed to go uptown and face her little girl. The body against which she would hold her Kathy had been shown naked to a roomful of men, for money. The shame ate away inside her like a corrosive acid.

When night came and The Mummy Case filled with men off the streets, off the canal barges and the Great Lakes steamers, she sat in the little dressing room listening to the waves of sound rolling against the closed door. Her hands went to her ears to blot out that pulsing throb, but the vibrations beat against her steadily like waves pounding at a beach.

A hand rapped on the door. The knob turned. The Egyptian slid inside, cheeks flushed and eyes overbright, holding the door slightly ajar so that now she could hear the sounds clearly.

"Give us the sleepytime girl!"

"Let's see the girl who gets ready for bed."

"Get those beef trust babes off the stage!"

"We want the woman with the long black hair."

54

The Egyptian whispered, "Can you hear them? Can you? If you don't go out there, they'll riot. They're getting in an ugly mood, I tell you. Look, Moira—I'll make it a hundred dollars. A century note just to go out there and do what you did last night. If they riot it'll cost me close to a thousand." The saloon owner's features were tight with concern.

Moira shivered. Now she caught the ugly note in the voices, the hard stamp of feet on the floor. Twice the piano missed its beat. There was terror in the air. She wanted no bloodshed on her account, no property smashed.

"All right! All right! I'll do it. Only to keep them from causing harm." Moira rose to her feet and began unbuttoning her dress. "Go ahead. Make an announcement. Give me ten minutes."

The Egyptian smiled and patted her shoulder. "Good girl. You won't regret this. And I meant it about the century note. Right after your performance, it's yours."

Her fingers were numb as she pushed the dress to her hips and down around her ankles. Fate was an evil genie, driving her further and further along an unseen road. She bit down hard on her lip, wondering where it would end.

Mike Gannón saw the flames even before the *Lucky Penny* docked alongside the Canal Street wharves. He stood by his helm, helpless, knowing one of his Lucky Line barges was afire and unable to do anything about it. He cursed monotonously between his clenched teeth as every muscle in his body sought to urge the barge faster through the water.

He left the helm when the starboard bumper hit a piling. He was across the deck, leaping a stretch of water, landing on the wharf. He could hear the sounds of fighting now, and the strident curses of angry men. He ran as if the devil nipped at his heels, eyes hard and bright, unfastening his pea jacket and throwing it to one side.

Three of his men were surrounded by a dozen brawny bullies, taking fists and axe handles across shoulders and faces. One of his men was down, stretched out with his battered features covered by a bloody froth. Another was on his knees, retching in an agony of smashed guts. As Mike came pounding along the wharf he saw a third man drop as the two remaining men stood back to back, flailing away with their fists.

He slammed into a couple of the roisterers, turning one

55

and driving a hard knee upward into his crotch. As the man screamed and fell away, Mike yanked the axe handle from his hand.

He used the length of wood like a club, driving it into two faces at once, seeing noses mashed flat and teeth spurt from crushed lips. His left arm he used as a brace, his tensed hand whirling men out of the way, giving himself room to swing the handle. He drove the wood across the back of a skull and against the front of a throat.

At sight of him his own men grew strong. Now they parted, choosing two men each, tackling them, knocking them into the street. Their fists hammered into jaws and cheeks. Mike was vaguely aware that he was mouthing thick, hot curses deep in his throat. These were Bennett men. He knew a couple of them. The red flames visible in the canal as the *Lucky Devil* was ravaged by fire added to the fury with which he used the axe handle.

Seven of the bullyboys were down now. Gannon dropped an eighth by clubbing his forehead. He swung around to continue the fight but the others were legging it up Canal Street.

Gannon dropped the axe handle and ran for a water bucket. There were no volunteer firemen in this section of the city. All a man could do was whisper prayers—or curses —and grab a pail of water.

"Five dollars to every man who gives me a hand," he roared to the tramps and loungers who had gathered to watch the fight. He leaped onto the deck of the barge, reaching for a tin pail.

His two bargemen came to help him, dropping roped buckets overside, lifting them, passing them to the volunteers who were forming a ragged line on the deck planks. They formed a bucket brigade, passing the pails from hand to hand until they came to big Mike Gannon who sent the water sloshing down into his burning hold.

The first few pails gave him room to stand below-decks. Now more volunteers came to earn drinking money. A bargeman dropped beside him, catching every other pail, sending water flying onto the flames.

"How did it happen, Joe?" Gannon panted.

"Don't know, boss. We say them coming off the barge. We ran to meet them. We left Bill Bradley on guard. They must've knocked him out. Soon as we met up with them we started scrapping."

"Bennett's boys. First a few fist fights, then a burning. After that more burnings—two at once, sometimes. Then he'll offer to buy me out. Damn his soul to hell! I'll make him pay for this!"

They worked on, with the flames scorching their shirts and trousers, with flying sparks singeing hair and burning naked flesh. Time hurried on until it was only an eternity of heat and splashing water and aching, cramping muscles. Mike Gannon stood on spraddled legs using his pails with cold fury, making every bucketful count.

It took them three hours, but they finally beat out the fire.

The barge was saved, but the Lucky Line had lost a cargo of fine leather gloves. Mike Gannon ran blackened fingers through his hair, trying to guess at the amount of his losses. Insurance might cover the gloves; he had none on the barge. Carpenters would have to work a week to make the *Lucky Devil* canalworthy again.

"Get what men we have in Buffalo," he rasped to his panting bargemen. "Get back here as fast as you can."

He went up on deck, glad to be out of the smoking, stinking hold. Reaching into his pocket he began peeling off dollar bills, counting them out to the volunteers. Then he went to look at his three men lying on the wharf. One of them would have to be hospitalized. The other two were sitting up, drinking brandy from a bottle.

"I'm paying Black John a visit, as soon as the others get here," he told them. "You boys are excused from—"

"Don't excuse me," growled one man, wiping blood from his lips with a tattered sleeve. "I got a score of my own to settle with them bastards."

"Count me in, too," said the second. "I took a handle on the head before I got a chance to blood my knuckles."

Gannon grinned. "There'll be bonuses paid out if we do Empire enough damage. You won't be sorry."

Thirty-seven men gathered on the still-warm planks of the *Lucky Devil's* deck. They were in an ugly mood. All of them had weapons of one kind or another, hammer handles, leather saps, police billies. Almost half had dull brass knuckles on their fists.

"No quarter," said Mike Gannon. "You smash everything that belongs to Black John Bennett. If we're not stopped by the coppers, I'll burn his place down around his ears."

There were no cheers, only throaty growls to answer him.

His eyes went from one face to another. The men were in an ugly mood. They wanted trouble this night for they were tired of being pushed about by Bennett musclemen.

"Come on," said Mike crisply. "Let's go after them."

They spread out across the street and men ran to get out of their way, wanting no part of this canawler feud. Silently they moved through the gathering shadows until they saw the wooden sign of the Bennett Enterprises offices ahead of them.

Mike Gannon came to a stop before the big wooden building and his voice lifted thick and blurred with anger. "Black John— it's Gannon! Step out here and fight me like a man and save your office if you can."

There was no reply to his shouted challenge, so Gannon took half a dozen quick steps forward and drove a heel at the door lock. Twice he kicked before the wood splintered. Then a shoulder hit its panels and the door burst inward.

"Wreck it," Mike growled.

His men went to work with axes and iron crowbars. Wood buckled. Chairs splintered. Pictures and shipping schedules came down off the walls to be ripped apart and added to the debris piled high in the middle of the big room. The men laughed and shouted as they worked. To them it was a huge game in which each one of them was a winner.

When the room was filled with wreckage, Mike threw kerosene over the debris and touched a sulphur tip to it. A roar of gases and a rising sheet of flame exploded together. In an instant the room was an inferno of fire and heat.

Gannon dismissed his men and stood alone, staring about him with hard eyes and grim face. Black John Bennett would need no calling card to tell him what had happened this night. From this instant on it was open war between Bennett and himself.

It was the way both of them wanted it.

On the stage of The Mummy Case, Moira Creegan was draping a thin nightgown above her head, letting it slide down about her white hips, back turned to the silent audience. As the silk whispered around her legs, she realized suddenly that she had not minded this second disrobement nearly as much as she had the first; then, she had been in an agony of embarrassment; now, she was somewhat more used to letting herself be stared at.

She turned and stretched and her eyes went over the eager,

58

gaping men crowding the long saloon. They were so hungry for her, it was almost amusing. On an impulse she lifted fingers to her lips and blew them a kiss before turning and running lightly across the stage into the wings where The Egyptian was standing.

The house shook with deafening applause. The maroon curtains were swinging shut but the hand-clapping and the foot-stamping went on and on.

The Egyptian said, "Go on out and take a bow. Give them another look at you."

Well, why not? Moira thought. She had let them see her without anything on. At least she was wearing the black nightgown now. She went to the center of the stage and pulled back the drapes, posing as calmly as any opera star. She made a deep curtsy, letting them see the white perfection of her body as far down as her navel.

Applause beat around her like gigantic wings.

The Egyptian bit her lip, staring through a gap in the curtain at the standing, shouting men. She could see a few of the local tavern keepers and saloon owners rising to their feet. Word of the new act had spread swiftly all along Canal Street. Chips Jorgensen was out there, heavy-set and wearing his perpetual derby, a cigar sticking out of his lantern jaw. There was Frenchy Duval, too, small but lithe and terrible in a knife fight, and Tank Andrews who owned The Yellow Rose.

The Egyptian chuckled throatily. It must be some show to attract rival cabaret owners. When she heard a footfall behind her she turned and saw Frenchy Duval and Tank Andrews approaching. Andrews was a big man, close to three hundred pounds.

"Howdy, ma'am," he said to Moira as she came from the stage to stand beside The Egyptian. "I'm Tank Andrews. I'll pay you fifty dollars a week to put on that same show in my Yellow Rose."

"Seventy-five," smiled Duval, making a little bow, eyes roving over the white body beneath the black silk nightgown. "Seventy-five dollars a week to strut your stuff at my Sidewalk Cafe."

The Egyptian pushed between them. "Easy, boys! Easy! Moira here belongs to me and The Mummy Case. I'm paying her a hundred a week with a percentage of the net take, so there's no need to waste your time." She was urging them toward the alley door.

59

A stagehand was handing Moira her clothes. The Egyptian hurried toward her. "I meant that about the hundred a week, you know. That's a lot of money to pay one woman. Think about it while you get dressed. I'll be waiting in my office with a contract."

"Oh, I couldn't," Moira said hurriedly. "I just couldn't."

"And why not?" a voice roared thickly. "You've shown off everything you own this night. Why not keep on doing it?"

"Mike!" cried Moira, and ran to meet him where he stood framed in the stage doorway.

His face was white with rage, his voice thick with the fury pulsing in his veins. "Have you no shame, girl? I offered to make you my wife a while back. Do you like this better than being Mrs. Mike Gannon?"

"Mike, I didn't want to—but the men were rioting. I was afraid someone would be hurt!"

"Ah, do you expect me to believe a tale like that?"

The contempt in his eyes stung Moira. Her chin tilted defiantly. "I'm not in the habit of lying, Michael Gannon."

"Is that so, now?"

"Yes, that's so! Lily, go fill out that contract. I'll be in to sign it directly."

Mike caught Moira's forearm. "I'm forbidding it, woman. Can you understand that?"

She laughed at him and wrenched herself free. "I don't belong to you, Mike Gannon. I don't belong to Rome or my dead husband's family, either. Now I belong to Canal Street."

CHAPTER FIVE

She stared up at him defiantly, fury glinting in her eyes, a lock of her black hair fallen down over a flushed cheek. Her heavy breasts stormed upward into the loosely held nightgown.

By God, she is a trull! Naked under the black silk and flushed from showing herself off to half a thousand men in the big room outside! A married woman with a child, yet with no more shame than any harlot off the streets!

60

His hand caught her wrist and his fingers tightened. "Canal Street woman, are you? All right, Moira Creegan—if this is the game you want to play, by God! I'll play it with you. Lily ought to have the contracts ready by now—let's go pay her a visit."

She yanked back but his fingers on her wrist were too strong. "At least let me dress," she panted.

His grin was mirthless. "Why dress? I like you as you are, naked under that nightgown. It shows off your legs something fierce." His hand went behind her and closed over a soft buttock, stroking it gently. When she fought to break free his laughter scratched at her. "A Canal Street woman knows better than to fight her man. Time you learned that."

"You're not my man, Mike Gannon!'

"Sure, you know better than that. But in case you don't, I'll teach the truth to you after you sign your agreement. Come along, now. Lily will be waiting in her cubbyhole of an office."

She went with him because she could not prevent herself from doing so, with his iron hand on her forearm and his great strength dragging her at a half-run. Anger pulsed in her veins at every step.

And yet . . . Moira Creegan realized that she was enjoying every moment of this manhandling. Half in shame, half in delight, she grew aware that her breasts had become hard and swollen with the sudden heat of desire that was in her.

He hurled her into the office so that she staggered and half fell over an easy chair. The Egyptian stared in surprise, first at Moira as the clothes went flying from her hand and she leaned awkwardly over the chair arm, then at Mike as he bulked huge and powerful in the doorway, breathing harshly.

"Sign the paper," he growled. "Write away your decency."

The Egyptian held out the pen after dipping it into an inkwell. Without taking her eyes off Mike, Moira scrawled her name at the bottom of the paper. Her hand flung the pen away as she turned to face the man in the doorway.

"There, it's done," she told him, head held high.

His grin was lopsided. "Lily, we'll borrow your bedroom this night. I'm paying a hundred dollars to your new employee for the privilege of spending the night with her."

"You wouldn't dare," Moira snapped.

"Och, and wouldn't I now?" He laughed and moved on

her. Moira retreated slowly, backing toward the rear stair doorway. Then Mike was on her, lifting her off her feet and swinging her to one side while he threw wide the door. Over his shoulder he said, "If she yells a little, don't be alarmed, Lily girl. It's only manners I'll be teaching her."

He slammed the door on an open-mouthed Egyptian.

Moira fought every step of the way but she was held like a child. "Mike, please—let me go. I don't want to—"

"I'm buying you this night, Moira. It's the only thing a Canal Street woman understands. It's time you learned it. Money and a man—or maybe I should have said, a man for money."

"You're hateful! You're like a—like some awful beast."

Mike was moving toward the open bedroom door. The woman in his arms was soft and warm, sweetly perfumed. She fought him, but her frantic squirmings only added to his hunger for her flesh.

"Mike, you must be joking. You've never been like this before. You were always sweet and gentle. Even that night on the barge, you were considerate. It's why I fell in love with you."

Amusement rumbled into laughter within him. "Love? What do you mean by that word, Moira Creegan? A woman in love will marry her man, and be proud to do it. But not you. I don't think you know the meaning of the word."

He stepped into the sitting room and crossed the thick Turkish rug to drop her on the Belter sofa. With legs spread, he glowered down at her. "So if you won't come to me for love, you'll come to me for money."

"I came to you on the barge, Mike," she reminded him, leaning forward, a hand outstretched pleadingly.

"Ah, and did you now? I have a recollection it was to thank me for your passage from Rome to Buffalo. You said something about it, I mind, as we played together in the bunk. Christ! I came near hitting you at the time."

He locked the door, then put the key in his pocket. From his coat he took a wallet, counted out ten ten-dollar bills, and placed them on the mantelpiece.

"Your fee," he told her crisply.

She flushed and came off the couch. "Mike, for the last time I'm going to appeal to your better nature. Don't do this thing to me. I've always thought we were good friends—all right, even more than that—"

"Save your breath, mavourneen," he told her.

62

His hands caught her shoulders and drew her to him. His lips touched her soft throat and moved down across the upper swells of her breasts. Moira felt his passionate need for her. He was a big man and heavily muscled, yet when he felt her softness against him, he trembled and his hands pressed into her smooth back.

"Show some life, girl," he growled. "A hundred dollars is a lot of money to spend on a Canal Street floozy."

"Make me," she told him calmly.

Gannon drew back and looked down at her, a queer grin twisting his lips. "So that's the way it's to be between us, is it?"

His hand bunched fingers in her thick black hair, freeing it from hairpins and combs, letting them shower down onto the rug. He shook out her hair, then gripped it tightly in his fingers, yanking back on it. Tears of pain sprang into her eyes.

"Mike, what are you doing?" she cried.

"Making you, sweetheart, as you asked."

Moira felt her neck tendons arch as her head was dragged back and back while her middle was forced forward. Her breasts lifted, pointing their stiff brown nipples at the ceiling. When she felt his lips touch them, she gave a soft cry.

"Mike! Oh, my God, Mike! I'll do it—whatever you want. Only no more of this. It makes me feel like a common streetwalker."

"You signed the paper. You said you belonged to Canal Street. I want to teach you what it means to be a Canal Street woman."

"I never knew it meant I'd be treated like this."

Her belly stirred against him, writhing gently. Mike gasped as realization came to him that Moira Creegan was enjoying his brutality, that the events of the past few days, in which she had given up her genteel way of life for the harsh reality of stripping naked before half a thousand men, required in her mind that she be punished. His hand in her hair was a part of that punishment, as was his savage manner.

His hand sought her hard breasts, gripping them tightly, one after the other. For several moments she endured the agony of his probing, before the ball of need in her middle burst its bonds. A wail of sound lifted from her open mouth. The breath rasped in her throat and became a harsh panting.

"Mike, you bastard! I never thought you'd ever be like

63

this. But I don't mind. I really don't. I like to be handled this way. I never knew I did but it's true. I'll be your Canal Street woman if you want it this way between us. I will, I promise I will. I'll give you your money's worth. Oh, Mike, Mike. . . ."

She was babbling words but Mike was certain she would never remember what she was saying. He was punishing her for the evil things she had done, and she was telling him how grateful she was, no more.

Then she lifted her hands to his face, stroking his cheeks. As his hand eased its grip in her thick black hair, she came hard against him, arms around his neck, open mouth hunting his lips hungrily, voraciously. He shook to the thrust of her tongue.

"Darling, darling," she whimpered. "Do you really like me to be a harlot? I don't mind at all. I've forgotten what it was like to be a gentlewoman. I'm Mike Gannon's Canal Street woman."

His hand caught the shoulder straps of the black nightgown and yanked them down. Her breasts burst into view, big and white, with turgid nipples betraying her need. She smiled as he bent to kiss her. Her eyelids flickered as she felt the touch of his tongue. She gasped and cried out softly.

"You, Mike. Take your clothes off. Please? Here—let me."

She moved her fingers lightly over him so that his shirt and coat came off together. His belt buckle was undone. Her hands pushed at his trousers. When he was naked she stepped out of her nightgown and held her arms out to him.

They came together in an explosion of need, forgetting time and identity in this gasping delirium. His hands sought her breasts, lifting them to his caresses. Gently his palms stroked her hips, her thighs. She gave him her own hands, as if to rouse him to a further madness. Her soft cries blended with his labored breathing. And then as they collapsed across the Belter sofa they joined one another in a timeless, ecstatic crucible of sheer sensation.

Much later they sought the bed in the next room and here again Mike drew her to him, kissing and caressing her until she moaned for him to take her again.

"I never meant all those things I said and did," he

64

whispered into her ear, nuzzling a path through the thick black hair.

"I know, I know," she soothed him. "You gave me the treasure of your love and you thought I was pulling it through mud. I understand, my darling. But you've got to understand me, too. I must be independent, by any means at all. I'm going to care for my baby. I've got to stand on my own feet. If the only way I can do it is by taking my clothes off downstairs before all those men—then I have to do it that way. . . ."

His kisses on her loose mouth halted her words. She gasped and clung to him. "Mike, I love you. I do—just as much as you love me. But I must be a person, can't you see? Because of what happened in Rome, I have to strike out for myself. Something inside is making me."

"I'll try," he whispered, moving closer to her warmth. "I will try, Moira. I promise. Only for now, be still. Only let your body speak to me."

The night closed in and united them in pleasure.

Morning sunlight woke Moira Creegan. She lay on her back, staring up at the ceiling of the bedroom for a little while before memory came to her. Rising on an elbow she bent over Mike, smiling tenderly as he slept on. She wanted to wake him. Her hand stretched out. And then she drew it back, blowing him a kiss with her fingertips, sliding naked from the bed and walking toward her clothes in the adjoining bathroom.

Bathed and dressed she moved past the bed where Mike still slept so soundly, tiptoeing now so as not to wake him. In the hallway, as she came through the kitchen, she heard hard voices in the big room. Curious, she opened the swinging door and stared out. A big man with black hair faced The Egyptian. A gold watch chain crossed his checkered vest. An unlit cigar was in his fingers as he gestured.

"I'll find him, Lily. It'll go easier on you if you play the game with me. Now for the last time—where's Gannon?"

Almost of its own volition, her hand pushed the door wide. "Mike Gannon?" Moira asked. "He's been gone for hours. I'd guess he left somewhere around four this morning."

They turned and considered her. Black John Bennett was scowling darkly. "Who're you?" he asked bluntly.

The Egyptian made a little gesture. "My new entertainer, John. If you'd been here last night you'd have seen her. She's going to be very popular along Big Ditch Street. Mike Gannon bought her favors for the night."

A long moment the big Irishman ran his hard eyes over Moira Creegan. She could read no emotion behind those eyes; it was as if he had drawn a curtain over them. She felt repelled by his stare, and now she could understand why Mike so despised and hated this man.

"He paid me a hundred dollars," she said suddenly.

Bennett grunted and turned away. He said to The Egyptian, "He'll be back to see her again. Next time, I'll be here."

"You keep your feuds outside The Mummy Case, John Bennett," the dusky woman said. "I won't have you making my place your battleground."

"He burned my offices down, early last night. I'll pay him back for that if it's the last thing I ever do. Anywhere I find him. Remember it, Lily."

He walked out of the saloon and into the early morning sunlight. Moira pursed her lips thoughtfully. This feud between Black John and her Mike was something no man or woman could prevent. It must run its course. If it drew Moira Creegan into its wild maelstrom of hate and violence, that was just too bad for Moira Creegan.

She shivered, running a hand up and down her arm.

Despite the glum attitude of Mike Gannon, Moira discovered as the days went by that she was growing quite content to be a Canal Street woman. Every night she took off her clothes before a crowded house, but once a week she hired a gig and drove to the Buffalo Savings Bank where she deposited an even one hundred dollars. Then she always drove on to the Jennings' boarding house to see Kathleen.

Kneeling, holding her sobbing child in her yearning arms, she knew that she was doing the right thing. She did not mind letting men see her body any more. The night with Mike in The Egyptian's sitting room had purged her of a sense of guilt. Besides she was doing it all for Kathy. She hugged her little girl and her smile was radiant as she told her that she planned to take her off on a picnic this afternoon to Jefferson Park.

"The child's an angel," Bertha Jennings enthused, accepting the three dollars which was the weekly fee for

Kathleen's food and lodging. "I declare, I look on her as my own." The woman hestitated then added, "She needs a mother, Mrs. Creegan. I know it's really none of my affair but—"

Moira nodded, smiling sweetly. "It isn't any of your affair, Mrs. Jennings. My husband is dead. My job requires that I travel constantly. I can only squeeze out these weekend visits. Believe me, if I could spend all my time with my baby, I would."

There was such a yearning in her voice that Bertha Jennings knew pity. She nodded and pressed a perfumed handkerchief to her nose. "I understand, dear. I try to take your place, you know, but it isn't the same. It really isn't."

They would go on their picnic, or sometimes it might be a drive in a gig out into the nearby countryside, to look at farm animals. Wherever it was, for a little while Moira could forget she was a Canal Street performer and revel in her role of mother. With Kathy, she could forget The Mummy Case.

Frenchy Duval was waiting for her outside her dressing room door, turning a watch fob around and around with his fingers, his eyes roving over her body. He had been leaning against the wall; he straightened as she approached and made her a little bow.

"I'll pay you two hundred simoleons a week, honey," he breathed. "I'm tired of seeing the crowds come into The Mummy Case night after night. I want those crowds spending money at my place."

Moira smiled at the small Frenchman. Two hundred dollars a week. Why, that was a fortune in these days when a girl could buy a fashionable summer straw hat for only seventy-five cents, and a dress for less than five dollars! Her heart began to pump excitedly. With two hundred dollars a week she could send Kathleen abroad to be educated and lay aside a small fortune for a dowry—

"Two hundred and fifty," a deeper voice said from the shadows of the hall. Moira swung around to see heavy-set Tank Andrews advancing on her, curiously light on his feet for all his bulk, showing his gold teeth in a wide, oily smile. His pudgy hand went to his hat, lifting it.

"Evening, ma'am. I overheard Frenchy making his pitch. I wanted to tell you, anything he offers, I'll go fifty dollars higher."

"Oh, dear," murmured Moira, staring from one to the other.

High heels sounded on the bare wooden floor. The Egyptian swept up with a swish of taffeta skirts, inclining her head a little to both men. "It seems I have to be everywhere these nights to keep my girls. What is it now, Tank? Frenchy?"

"We're after this girl, none of the others," rasped Duval.

"And we're prepared to pay her, jointly—she can spend one week at The Yellow Rose, one week at The Sidewalk Cafe, eh, Frenchy?—the princely sum of three hundred dollars per week. Match that, Lily."

The Egyptian opened her mouth. She looked at Moira, then at the two men. Her smile was tight with restrained rage. "You both know what you're doing, of course. You're driving me out of business."

The little Frenchman shrugged his shoulders with elaborate politeness. *"Oui,* we know very well. You're doing the same thing to us. Business has fallen off to a whisper since this *belle putaine* has been slipping into her silk nightie on your stage. We want our trade back. And yours with it, if it has to be that way."

Moira hugged her gown to her bosom, eyes touching the two men and the frightened, angry Egyptian. Three hundred dollars a week? It was unbelievable! She wondered what The Egyptian would do.

And then she found herself taking a step forward, saying, "Lily has already made me a better offer than that, haven't you, honey?"

The idea had come to her out of the blue. It would be a step upward in her social status here on Canal Street if The Egyptian would agree to her plan. Three hundred a week? She could make five hundred, maybe a thousand. It all depended on the frowning woman who was staring at her in puzzlement.

As if she sensed the help Moira offered, Lily nodded. "That's right, boys. I did make her an offer. She said she wanted time to think it over."

"Will you do better than three century notes?" sneered the heavy-set Andrews. "Frenchy and I can do it only by pooling our money."

Moira smiled. "Lily offered me a partnership."

The Frenchman stared blankly, "A partnership? You

mean she's actually turning over half of—ah, I don't believe it."

"Come on, Frenchy," Tank Andrews said. "We'll sit back and wait out developments." He moved toward the alley door, then turned with a flourish. "Your good health, ladies. Let me know a few weeks from now how you're getting along. Maybe Frenchy and I will get the stripper yet—at a somewhat reduced rate, of course, when The Mummy Case goes bust."

Frenchy Duval shifted uneasily, lifted his hands expressively, and went after him with rapid, mincing strides.

The Egyptian drew a deep breath. "You think just because you got me with my rump in a sling you can ask anything and get it."

Moira hardly heard her. She was hugging her gown, eyes dreaming. "Oh, relax, Lily. The idea came from nowhere but I've been standing here thinking about it. A partnership wouldn't be so bad—but we'd have to do something about The Case. Redecorate, for one thing. Buy the house next door and enlarge."

"Are you crazy?" the dusky woman howled.

"No, no. Listen, come into my room. I think we have hold of a gold mine. Oh, come on—will it hurt you to listen?"

The Egyptian pouted sullenly, but she went into the tiny dressing room and watched as Moira tossed her clothes over a standing screen and sat down at her vanity bench. For a moment she fluffed her thick black hair, then swung around to look at Lily.

'There were some very well dressed men in here tonight, weren't there?"

Lily shrugged casually. "We get them from time to time. There's been more than usual lately. I guess that's on account of you. Some of them are important people— bankers, newspaper editors, stock brokers, real estate men."

Moira leaned forward excitedly. "That's just my point. We'll redecorate The Mummy Case and give it another name. Something elegant, to attract the posh trade. But for the toffs we have a separate room, a place where they can be safe from the cruder element."

The Egyptian bit her lower lip. Against her will and contrary to her own better judgment, she found herself responding to the excitement of the other woman. A sin palace for the society swells, as part of the refurbished Mummy Case. She was woman of the world enough to know that men were the same when it came to women, whether they wore patched pants or evening clothes. The only difference was in their approach. She was making a good living from The Case, of course, but the society men had the money, no doubt of that; they would order champagne and Scotch, not beer or cheap whiskey. And there was money in liquor.

"Goddamn you, Moira," she said affectionately. "I was enjoying my life until you got me all stirred up about this idea of yours."

"You like it, then?"

"Hell, yes. Who wouldn't? We'd have a chance to be big —really big. But what a lot of work it will be! Two establishments to buy for, to supervise."

"More girls to hire, more accounts to be made out, more food and more liquor to be bought—but a lot more money to be made." Moira pondered. "We'd have to have cards printed, of course—passports to our society section. We'd have to sign them and pick and choose the men among whom to distribute them. No riffraff behind the velvet ropes, Lily. Only high society. Men with money to spend."

The Egyptian frowned. "Could you do a couple of shows a night? One for the main room, one for this other place?"

Moira stretched white arms high above her head. "For money, Lily, I can do anything." She lowered her arms and held out her hand. "Is it a deal—partner?"

The Egyptian caught her hand and squeezed it.

Business went on as usual at The Mummy Case. Only during the day was there frenzied activity as hordes of carpenters and plumbers, interior decorators and mechanics invaded the premises. By offering a bonus to every working-man, Moira got the job done. There were no lay-offs, no work stoppages. Not a single complaint was heard about coming into Canal Street to do a job. If they did their work within a two-week period, there was an extra bonus.

At first The Egyptian objected to this lavish spending but when she became aware that a dollar spent now might mean ten or twenty dollars a month from now, she grew more demanding than Moira. She would spend hours in the Annex, as they called the house they had taken over, watching walls being knocked down to permit the extension of hallways, supervising the building and furnishings of small rooms where rich clients might take some of the entertainers, if they were so inclined.

Moira had a suite of rooms made for herself in the new building which duplicated those of The Egyptian. She let interior decorators furnish it, too busy to check materials and color effects. The nights were taken up with her act and with projected new ones, since she reasoned that regular customers might grow tired of seeing her against a bedroom background all the time. Her days were filled with the sounds of hammering and sawing.

From time to time the women met and exchanged ideas.

The Annex was to have walls covered with red brocade and gilded woodwork. Its floor was to be tiled. A gigantic mirror was installed along the wall behind the bar. There would be no oil painting of a nude woman—too many saloons were so decorated. The décor was sedate, with elegance its keynote. A toff from fashionable Niagara Square or Deleware Avenue must be made to feel at home here so that he might indulge his whims against a background with which he was completely familiar. A man must be comfortable before he felt like sinning.

Cards were printed in black lettering on gold paper. Both Moira and The Egyptian inked their names on each individual card. They sent word into the city above The Terrace that these cards would be distributed among influential, well-to-do gentlemen only. The response appalled even Lily. "I never guessed there were so many bored men in Buffalo," she commented, and began to dream of greater wealth.

"All we need now is an opening night attraction," Moira murmured thoughtfully. "I've been playing around with a different act for the old stage. I thought I might put it on as a sort of tryout, to see what kind of reception it gets."

"What kind of act?" asked Lily.

Moira winked. "I want you to be surprised, honey. That way you can give me an honest opinion."

The name of the new entertainment palace was to be The Golden Tassel. A huge chandelier of gilded glass in the shape of a mighty tassel dominated the huge main room. The motif was repeated in the wall woodwork, along the seventy-foot mahogany bar, and on the mirrors. It was to be a kind of trademark. Moira wanted to work it into her act but she could not think of a way, as yet.

71

"I'll put on my tryout act tonight on the old stage. Be sure to catch it. Let me know what you think of it," she said to The Egyptian.

The grand opening was two nights away.

Morgan Davies found The Mummy Case entirely by accident.

He was in Buffalo on a legal matter, representing the firm of Davies, Summerville and Atkins for his Uncle Phineas. A young man in his early twenties, recently out of Harvard Law School, he intended to specialize in corporation law. For some time he had been considering making a break with the firm and striking out for himself. Rome was too small for the kind of legal work he had in mind, so he was combining personal with firm business while in Buffalo, making inquiries around the city to learn what opportunities might be available for his immediate future.

No libertine, he was nevertheless inclined to kick over the traces every once in a while. He had heard of Canal Street and the vices it offered for money. Discreet mention of its name brought amused smiles and fatherly advice from the older lawyers he was visiting.

He ignored the advice as he ignored the smiles.

Dusk lay across the canal as Morgan Davies wandered the cobblestoned length of Big Ditch Street. His eyes were drawn to one establishment after another, but he rejected them all. He came opposite The Mummy Case just as a brougham drew up and three men dressed as neatly as himself stepped out, paid the driver and walked in through the glass doors.

Morgan Davies pondered. The Mummy Case seemed all right. The three young men who had just entered were his own kind. If this place was acceptable to them, it must rank as a better sort of saloon. Certainly it would do no harm to enter it, if only for a beer.

The bartender was friendly. As he pushed a frothing glass across the bar top, he said, "Show goes on in a few minutes. Moira's putting on a new act tonight. Place is pretty jammed but you might find room if you act fast."

"She pretty?"

"We don't get crowds like this for no old hag, that's for sure. Go on, take a look. Maybe you'll like her enough to come back again."

Carrying his refilled beer mug, he moved toward the

stage hall. The place was crowded, all right. Must be upwards of five hundred men packed in at the tables. But luck was with him. He found an empty chair a dozen feet from the stage.

He sipped his beer and when that was done he ordered a pitcher. The gas lamps were being lowered—the orchestra began to play. A thrill of excitement chased down his spine in response to the obvious electricity in the air.

The curtain went back with a faint swish of material.

The stage showed a bathing beach, with painted water in the background. A bathing wagon had been placed in the middle of the stage—a four-wheeled cart which could be rented at beaches for bathers to change in. The entire wall facing the audience had been cut away, giving a perfect view into the interior.

A woman walked onto the stage, parasol twirling in her fingers, smiling faintly. She was dressed in the height of fashion, in a somewhat tight princess dress which hugged her full bosom and slim waist, the skirt of which was gathered by a drapery between knees and high-buttoned shoes. Her heavy black hair was coiffed high on her head. The woman paused a moment, staring at the painted backdrop as if considering a dip in the inviting ocean waters.

Then she ran lightly across the stage to the wooden steps of the bathing cart, collapsing her parasol as she went.

Morgan Davies had risen half out of his chair.

"Sit down there," somebody yelled.

"Of course, of course. Sorry," young Davies muttered.

Dazed, he sank back into his seat. The woman in the bathing cart was nobody else but Mrs. Creegan. Moira, the barkeep had said. Certainly! Mrs. Moira Creegan. He had seen her often enough at society gatherings in Rome. She and her husband had been to his parents' home more than once. He had even listened while she played the piano.

Now she was within twenty feet of him and—

Morgan Davies swallowed. His throat was very dry. She was unbuttoning the princess dress down the back. God in heaven! Did she mean to take off her clothes right here in public, in full view of five hundred men? He could not believe it.

This was like peeping into the window of a neighbor's house and watching the lady of the house removing her garments. Realization burst on him belatedly that this was exactly the suggestion Mrs. Creegan was making on the stage. He and the other men with him were permitted to see a woman preparing to put on her bathing suit, one of those awkward woolen affairs that would so effectively hide her from throat to knees.

The princess dress was being pushed down to her hips, revealing the fact that she was wearing a thin linen chemise with white lace on its shoulder straps and at the bodice. Under the linen her full breasts moved loosely, quivering to the movements of her bare arms. First one stockinged leg and then the other was raised to permit her to step from the crumpled dress. The chemise clung tightly to her hips; as she bent over, her buttocks pressed into the tight material, printing their outline for all to see.

Morgan Davies felt the room and the men in it slip away. He was aware only of Mrs. Creegan in the bathing cart as she stretched her arms high above her head and wriggled a little in delight at being free of the tight confines of the princess dress. He had always assumed himself to be a respectable young man. Watching a woman remove her clothing was exciting enough, but when he knew that woman personally, not as a public entertainer but as the respected wife of a now-deceased client, excitement was a mild word for the delight which flooded him. It was almost as if he were enjoying an assignation with her in the bath cart.

The lace-edged shoulder straps came down her arms. Then she lowered the chemise to her middle, baring the magnificent white breasts with their full, rounded nipples. She crossed the cart like that, her naked breasts shaking ripely, to lift down a woolen bathing suit from the wooden wall peg where it had hung. She came back across the room, humming faintly.

Morgan Davies wondered what Elvira Tomkins and Martha Creegan would say to the news that their sister-in-law was putting on an indecent performance in the city of Buffalo. Lately they had been coming into the office with demands that Davies, Summerville and Atkins locate Moira Creegan and institute proceedings against her so they could take little Kathleen away from her.

The hell with Elvira Tomkins and Martha Creegan! I refuse to work for the firm during off hours, when my time's my own. And how better might I spend it—since I came down to Canal Street on the prowl for excitement—than by watching respectable Mrs. Creegan taking off her clothes?

Moira was pushing the chemise past her hips. Now her

74

back was turned to the audience, naked except for black silk stockings and high-buttoned shoes. She shook out her chemise and folded it carefully. There was no sound in the big room as she turned and lifted the bathing outfit, holding it up as if to gauge its size.

The orchestra was playing muted music.

One white leg lifted to thrust into the bathing suit, and then the other. Bit by bit those shapely legs were disappearing behind gray cotton. She was wriggling sinuously, tugging the suit past her hips and on upward to veil the heavy breasts.

Buttoning the shoulder straps, she opened the door and ran lightly down the cart steps and across the stage to the wings. As she disappeared, the big room exploded with sound. Men yelled and clapped, whistling shrilly. Their heavy brogans drummed the floor. Morgan Davies yelled right along with them, standing now and waving an empty beer mug over his head.

The Egyptian threw her arms about a smiling Moira Creegan.

"Darling, you were utterly sensational! If anything, it was better than the bedroom scene. There wasn't even any standing room left. Did you notice?"

"I was too busy concentrating on what I was doing. I wanted to *be* a woman preparing for a swim, not just act like one."

"You were. Oh, you were! Listen to them!"

"I don't know, though. I don't think it's quite right for The Golden Tassel. We want something a little different, something with—well, the only word I can think of is 'class'. Something in the grand manner."

"All I can say is, if you can top your performance tonight, I'll buy drinks for the house out of my own pocket."

Moira patted her cheek. "Angel! Can't talk any more. Got to go take a bow. See you later."

She ran out onto the stage and blew kisses to her audience, smiling down into their upturned faces. A few short months ago she would have died with shame for what she had done tonight in front of them. Repetition brought its own anodyne. She guessed she was growing tougher, here in Canal Street. She was no longer the helpless widow. She was able to stand on her own two feet now.

For a moment, as her eyes ran over the audience, she

75

thought her heart might stop. One face seemed to leap out at her. Morgan Davies.

A swirl of men went past him, hiding him from view. She told herself she must be mistaken. A fine young man like Morgan Davies would never enter a place like The Mummy Case. She *must* be mistaken! The young man she had seen bore a startling resemblance to Phineas Davies' nephew, that was all.

She turned and ran off the stage, suddenly frightened.

CHAPTER SIX

The stone hit the building wall a few inches above his head, bringing Mike Gannon around on a brogan heel, arm lifted to protect his face from further flying rocks. Three men stood facing him, tough canalers in thick woolen sweaters, big grins on their faces. Bennett men, picked for their ability to rough and tumble.

"We were sent to fetch you, Gannon," one man said.

"On your own feet or on ours," another added.

The third man chuckled. "The choice is yours, matey."

"Fetch me where?" Mike rasped.

"Black John wants to see you. In the alleyway behind The Bloody Deck. He has words to say to you."

Gannon lifted his thick-set shoulders in a shrug. No sense wasting his strength on these toadies, if Bennett was thinking of having him beaten up. He might need all his muscles for what was to come. He stepped forward, watching the three canalers draw back.

"At least you're respectful of your betters," he told them, and was pleased to see the hot anger in their eyes. "All right, my bullyboys. Lead the way."

They walked at a brisk pace up Canal Street. Gannon strode with his eyes fastened to their wide backs, wondering what deviltry Black John planned for him. An imp of stubbornness was in the big Irishman at the moment. His knuckles itched for action. He only hoped Bennett might be feeling the same tempestuous desires, but he supposed that would be too much to expect. Bennett wasn't one to fight his own battles.

They turned into the alleyway almost as one man. Mike Gannon came to a halt.

Black John was fifty feet from him, stripped to his middle, wearing trousers and shoes, talking to two of his cronies. One of his three guides motioned him closer. "Black John's waiting, Gannon. Or are you afeared to face him?"

Mike swung a vicious left hook. His fist connected solidly. The man went backwards into the building wall, poised there a moment with a foolish expression on his face, then slid down to the ground. Mike nodded in an almost friendly fashion to the others. "Shall we get on so as not to keep Mr. Bennett waiting?"

They stared truculently at Mike, then at their fallen fellow. One of them shrugged, chuckling. "Come along, Black John will do our work for us."

Bennett came to meet him, walking easily. His chest was deep and muscles flexed like cable on his midriff and upper arms. A thick hate began to work in Mike Gannon. This man held himself a step above the rest of the canawlers, deeming himself too good for the common run of Big Ditch men. It would be good to humble him, to knock him down into the alleyway dust, flat on his face, and watch him twitch.

"I'll give you one last chance, Gannon," Black John was saying as he approached. "I'll pay fifty thousand dollars for the Luck Line—cold cash within the hour."

"Save your breath, you black spalpeen," Gannon growled. "What's the real reason you sent for me?"

"To make you an offer. Then to pound some sense into that stupid skull of yours." Bennett saw the other man look around suspiciously. "No, no—no funny business. With my own fists. Just the two of us."

"You mean that?" Mike asked, incredulously.

Bennett smiled coldly. "Did you think I got where I am by hiding behind other men?"

Mike lifted his thick gray sweater off over his head. Naked to the waist now, he lifted his big fists. Bennett held up a hand. "I've posted men at either end of the alley. We won't be interrupted. Shall we make it a sporting thing between us? If I knock you cold, you'll sell the Luck Line to me— for forty thousand."

"Agreed, by God. And if I lay you out?"

"I'll indemnify you for all the damages I've caused, with a bonus of ten thousand dollars above damages."

77

"You're mad," growled Gannon. "I'll make mincemeat of you."

Bennett laughed. "Try it, man—just try it."

The big Irishman should have been warned by the confidence of his opponent, but all he could see was the mocking smile on Bennett's face and the uplifted fists as the man posed like a prize fighter on a cigarette card. An urge to knock the smile from the arrogant face brought Gannon forward at a run.

Bennett seemed only to shift his feet but he was out of the way of Mike's bull-like rush and his left was whipping into Gannon's face. The big Irishman felt himself shaken from heels to head. He came around, throwing a looping right. Bennett stepped inside it and rammed a fist into his guts. The breath exploded from Mike's lungs. He backpedalled, panic touching him. A heavy fist rammed his ribs. He was being hurt, but the greatest emotion he felt was surprise. The fact that Black John Bennett was so quick with his fists and no mean opponent, seemed to paralyze the big Irishman.

Two fists thudded into his face, shaking him.

Mike threw a straight left, felt it jar home. He followed it with a cross to the jaw. Bennett went back on his heels. Instantly Mike was after him like a big wildcat hunting a wounded deer. He came up short as Black John pumped three jabs in his face.

Blood was streaming from his nose, making a salt taste on his puffed lips. Anger was a thickness in his limbs, making him slow. He had to shake off the fury. Then maybe he could rouse himself out of this lethargy which gripped him. Mike Gannon began to fight back.

Twice he rocked Bennett, heard him gasp and pant. But Black John was no fool. He stood little chance against Gannon in a free-for-all. His strength lay in his boxing skill. Bennett jabbed and ducked, hit and retreated.

Gannon went after him, shuffling through the dust, his nosebleed covering the thick hairs of his chest with crimson liquid. His cheek and his lips were puffy. Every time Black John hammered a fist into them, they hurt like hell. But he was marking the other man now. Slowly he was getting through his defenses, splitting Black John's lip, marking an eye with a shiner.

If he could get him soreheaded enough, Black John might forget his fighting style and stand toe to toe with

78

him, slugging it out. A right to the jaw made big Mike falter. He shook his head, moving backward, letting Black John come to him, meeting his jabs with solid blows that missed more often than they landed. But when they landed, they hurt.

Through his clouding senses he heard the shrill blast of a police whistle and he became aware that Bennett was trying to break free of the fight, snarling and swearing viciously. "It's the paddy wagon, man," Black John grated.

Gannon lowered his fists. "The Black Maria? What do they want?"

Bennett was turning away. He said over his shoulder, "Us, what else? We've been making noise enough to rouse the dead from their graves. Somebody must have heard and sent in the alarm."

It was an anticlimax. Gannon stood with his arms by his sides, watching his men run up to Bennett, lifting his discarded shirt and coat and then hotfooting it beside him up the alley.

Mike could hear the clipclop of the horses' hoofs, the louder shrilling of the police whistles. Quickly, he put on his sweater and legged it up the alleyway in Black John Bennett's dust.

The thought came to him as he ran that he and Bennett had settled nothing by their fight. Things were still the same between the Luck Line and Black John. He wondered when and where Bennett would strike at him again.

Frank Bannerman put his imported Havana cigar between his teeth and leaned toward the match The Egyptian was holding. He puffed contentedly, enjoying the aroma of the tobacco, his middle filled with filet mignon, the taste of champagne on his tongue. He leaned back and gestured at the room around him.

"A masterpiece, Lily. I'd never have believed it possible."

She smiled down at him, then let her eyes touch the red brocadework and gilded wood of The Golden Tassel. It was opening night. More than one hundred men in evening clothes were crowded at its tables and along the bar, and more were entering through the plate glass doors.

"I got to hand it to Moira," she said admiringly. "It was all her idea. She had to practically hit me over the head before I saw the light. I was satisfied with The Mummy Case. The more fool, me."

Bannerman calculated a moment, then nodded. "You ought to gross a quarter of a million dollars yearly at the prices you charge. Not that they're too exorbitant for what you offer, mind."

"You haven't seen anything yet," she laughed. "Wait until the show begins. Then you'll see the real reason why we're so positive society folks won't mind the high tariff it costs to come here."

"This new partner of yours, she's the one who did that bedroom skit?"

"She has a better routine worked out for The Tassel."

Bannerman pursed his lips. He was in his middle thirties, a highly successful real estate operator. He sold a lot of property in and around Buffalo and much of the money he made from his deals went into other profitable ventures. There was talk around the city that Frank Bannerman might run for State Senator in the coming elections. He was a man with money and influence.

A tall man, handsome in a florid manner, he had married one of the Tracy girls who brought her own wealth to match his, insuring them a top spot as society leaders.

"I'd like to meet this partner of yours, Lily," he said slowly. "It strikes me she has a head on her shoulders." He looked up quickly. "Does she know I own these buildings?"

"I never told her. I figured it was none of her business. I guess she thinks I own them, though she's never said anything about it."

"I'd rather you didn't tell her, not yet at any rate, until I can sit down and have a nice long chat with her. The *Courier* has been agitating to print the names of the owners of these Canal Street sin palaces. A few men and myself have been putting some pressure to stop it."

He cleared his throat. "Nothing wrong with owning property on Canal Street, obviously. Just the same, to a man in my social position in the city—you do understand, don't you?"

The Egyptian smiled and nodded. One of the waiters was beckoning. She made her apologies and left the table. Bannerman sat back and puffed at his cigar, nodding occasionally to an acquaintance whose eye he caught.

A smart move by this Moira Creegan, opening The Golden Tassel. Half of Buffalo—those men who counted, at least—were here at the grand opening. The rest would come tomorrow or the next night. The city has needed a place like this for a long time. Good place to bring customers to, excellent steak, the best wines and champagnes. Make a man feel important, just sitting here . . .

His thoughts were interrupted by the tapping of a conductor's baton. Bannerman settled himself more comfortably in his chair. He had an excellent view of the deep stage which occupied the north end of the room, all across one wall. If the performance lived up to half of what The Egyptian had suggested, the girls had a gold mine working for them.

The lamps dimmed. The curtain rustled back.

Frank Bannerman sat up, finding himself staring at a Roman bath. A scholar of sorts, he fancied himself an expert on ancient cultures. At first glance the simulated stone arches and the beveled edge of the pool seemed highly accurate as to detail. Just when he was settling himself to a consideration of a small room which was obviously the *alipterium* where expensive oils were massaged into the flesh of the bathers—surely those were earthenware oil jars, standing so neatly along the wall—his eye was caught by a shapely young girl who came running onto the stage. In her hand she carried sticklike objects—*strigils,* he understood suddenly, to rub the accumulated dirt and grime off the bodies of the bathers.

The young girl was a slave, then. All she wore was a twist of linen to shield her loins. In a moment two other slave girls joined her, also carrying *strigils.* Ah, of course. The room where they were standing was an *apodyterium* in which Roman ladies disrobed. They would be attended by slaves who would follow them into the *alipterium* to massage oil into their skins, then to the *tepidarium* to hold towels in which to encase them when they were done bathing. Bannerman shook his head in amazement.

Two Roman matrons emerged from the stage wing and entered the *apodyterium.* The slave girls came and began to remove their garments. The room was very still as the tableau was acted to its conclusion.

Applause burst out as the curtain closed.

Bannerman reached for his champagne goblet and drained it. His cheeks were flushed, his heartbeat accelerated. Moira Creegan and The Egyptian had an ideal setup here in The Golden Tassel. They had *carte blanche* along Canal Street to do what they would; no police force would come running to close their shows; they were avoiding the crude sex performances of their neighbors, and giving their educated customers a gilded, refined, though erotic, stage presentation.

He was well aware of the fact that he would share their good fortune to some extent. His monthly rentals were secure. It was with a warm, satisfied feeling in his middle that he lifted and sipped the cold wine as the curtain rustled back a second time.

A campfire glowed off to one side, probably a specially made gas fixture, but realistic enough, surely, for it cast red lights across a gaudily painted gypsy wagon and a dozen swarthy gypsy men and women.

The wagon door opened and a woman clad in brightly colored blouse and a short skirt of red linen stepped into view. Around her slim middle was twisted a belt of golden rope which held a huge gold tassel at her hip. Long black hair hung straight down over her shoulders. Huge gold hoops dangled from her ears. Her dusky face was beautiful, with large mouth wet with red lip salve, eyebrows arched and darkened, the eyes brightly glittering. Her feet were bare, the ankles banded about with tiny bells on silver chains.

The mandolins strummed furiously.

The gypsy came down the few steps of the wagon ladder with conscious grace, hips swaying languidly. Beneath the flowered blouse her breasts bulked large and firm, moving ripely to her stride. In pantomime the nomads grouped about the campfire pleaded with her to dance. Haughtily she refused, head high.

A big man came out of the shadows. His hand caught the flowered blouse and ripped it down her back so that it hung by a thin thread at a shoulder. A single pale breast was exposed between the torn remnants of the blouse. The same hand caught her elbow, whirling her, throwing her roughly to the ground.

For a moment she crouched, head lifted, lips drawn back to show gleaming white teeth, while every man in the audience thrilled to the savage hate reflected in her face. Then her shoulders began to move, gently at first, while harsh laughter poured from her open mouth. She grasped the gaudy shirtwaist and ripped it from her. Slowly she lifted to her feet, naked breasts swaying, shoulders rippling.

The mandolins went wild with pagan music.

And the woman danced . . .

82

She was a woman wronged by a man. To the warm summer night she showed her breasts, silently asking if these were delights to be ignored by the one she loved. In a dozen different ways she flaunted them, making them dance, lifting them in cupping palms. Like a forest dryad she floated about the stage, touching this man and that among the gypsies, crying out as their hands lifted to stroke her flesh, stamping her feet and whirling so that her long black hair flew wide.

Then her hand balled a corner of the red linen skirt and ripped it free. Naked except for the golden rope at her middle and the golden tassel hanging below it, she posed, a slim white arm lifted high, eyes challenging as they went over the gypsies, then over the breathless audience. Her hips shifted in rhythm to the muted music, gently at first, then swiftly. The long white legs were moving now, carrying her this way and that about the campfire, while her hands invited all eyes to the loveliness of her naked, mature beauty. This was the body her lover scorned.

Her lover was mad, was he not? To ignore these smooth white thighs, these shifting, thrusting hips, any man must be insane.

With shrill cries the gypsies urged her on.

Drunk with her own beauty in the summer night, the gypsy woman lost herself in the movements of the saraband. Head thrown back she arched her proud breasts under the eyes of the big man who had torn her blouse. While she laughed bitterly, her hips flailed the air before the onlookers. She was motion, from her long black hair to the painted red toenails on her feet.

Every eye in the great room was fixed on the naked woman on the stage. At his own table, Frank Bannerman was finding it hard to breathe. Never in his life had he seen such a display of raw emotion. His collar pinched his neck. The blood pounded furiously in his veins. He felt himself drawn up in the dance as if he were one of the gypsy men she taunted.

Then the woman was sliding bonelessly to the ground.

The mandolins stilled. The curtains swished closed.

Behind the protection of the closed curtains, Moira snatched up her torn blouse and red linen skirt and ran across the stage. The Egyptian was waiting in the wings, calling out congratulations.

83

"Just listen to them out there, just listen!" she cried, eyes feverishly bright. "We're in, honey—we're *in!* Word of your dance will be all over Buffalo within a day. We'll have to turn them away at the doors."

Moira extended her flushed cheek for a kiss, then ran for her dressing room. Exultation was a rising flood in her body. Laughter was quick to bubble on her lips. Success meant money in the bank for Moira Creegan and her little girl. The Buffalo that had refused her a job short months before would make her a wealthy woman before she was done with it.

Her hand closed the door of her tiny dressing room. She tossed the torn shirtwaist and red linen skirt through the air. Naked, she stared at her reflection in the standing mirror. A slow flush tinted her cheeks. A year ago she would have died rather than do the things she had done tonight. Now it did not seem to matter. It was as if she had become a different woman, deep inside.

The door opened behind her.

Startled, she whirled. "Mike," she cried happily, running toward him. Too late she saw the disgust and loathing in his eyes. The flat of his hand came up against her cheek, driving her reeling backward.

"You filthy whore," he rasped. "Have you no shame at all?"

"Mike, I—"

"To dance like that so everybody and his brother in Buffalo can see what you hide behind your clothes—"

Anger flickered to life in Moira Creegan. "They wouldn't give me a decent job, everybody and his brother, so I take their money the only way I can."

"Money, money, money! Is this the world to you?"

"Not to me, no. But for my Kathleen, yes."

"I have enough money for you and Kathleen, more than enough. For the last time I'll ask you, will you marry me and come away from all this?"

"I thought we'd reached an agreement, you and I, Mike. I believed I'd made you understand why I go on the stage."

"To watch you dance the way you did—I had to go out on the street and breathe the stinking air of Canal Street as a sweet change from what was happening on that stage."

Her palm came up hard against his cheek. Fury glittered in her eyes. Her lips twisted scornfully. "Get out of here,

Mike Gannon. Get out and never come back. I don't want to see you, ever again."

"Just like that, is it? Go away, after all we've been to one another. Walk out of your life as if I were a door-to-door salesman, peddling pots and pans."

Tears stung her eyes. "I w-won't listen to your constant scoldings. Why can't you accept me as I am? God knows I'm good enough to you in my bed upstairs. Any time you want, I'm there for you. Isn't that enough, Mike Gannon? I'm not carrying your name. I'm disgracing no one except myself."

He groaned. "It's that which eats in me! To see you dancing in your skin before those society swells rankles me like a boil before it breaks."

They stared at one another, and Moira could read the hunger and the love which looked out at her from his eyes. A little core of tenderness blossomed inside her. On naked feet she moved toward him, putting her arms about his middle and resting her cheek on his chest.

"Oh, Mike, Mike. Let's not fight. Can't you just accept what I do as proof that I love my daughter? I'm doing it for her, not for myself."

Emotion made him swallow. Under his palms her back was smooth and warm. He held her against him protectingly, biting back the hard, harsh condemnation that quivered for freedom on his tongue.

"Sure, I'm a bull in a china shop," he said at last. "I love you so much I hate to see you lower yourself this way. All right, all right. I won't say another thing about it."

His hands caught her shoulders, pushed her back and away from him. A scowl blackened his sun-bronzed face, "I'll be after getting out of here now, to let you get dressed."

"Wait for me in my rooms, Mike? Please?"

There was a little girl eagerness in her eyes that touched him. He felt like a bully when Moira Creegan looked up at him so appealingly. If ever he could talk some sense into her beautiful head!

"I'll wait," he growled, and moved toward the door.

In the hall he saw The Egyptian deep in conversation with a society toff, a handsome man in a black cloth Chesterfield overcoat, an Ascot scarf fluffed up beneath his chin, his gray and black striped trousers immaculately pressed. His face was vaguely familiar to Gannon. He had seen him be-

85

fore at The Mummy Case; Banners or something like it, his name was. The big Irishman brushed by them with a curt nod on his way to the stairs.

He did not see them turn and look after him.

"A close friend of hers?" asked Bannerman.

"Close enough. He's the one sent her to me. They used to be sweethearts on the canal before she married some Rome industrialist."

"Mmmm. Gone on him, is she?"

The dusky woman trilled laughter, squeezing his forearm. "I'm not so sure about that. Mike's a handsome devil, big and strong, but they're always fighting. He doesn't want her to go on the stage. She keeps insisting it's the only way she can support herself."

A rival for her favors, Bannerman thought, *if I decide to go that far with Moira Creegan.* There were ways of dealing with big, strong, stupid men. Frank Bannerman had availed himself of these methods during his rise to power. One more victim of a set of brass knuckles or a leaded billy. No man to worry himself over, that was for sure.

He nodded almost imperceptibly. "Take me in to meet her, Lily. I think it's time your partner and I were introduced."

The Egyptian tapped on the closed door. In answer to a muffled voice she called, "Company, honey. Somebody wants to meet you pretty badly."

Her hand turned the knob. The door went inward. Frank Bannerman let his eyes touch the woman in the thin silk wrapper seated before the vanity mirrors. She turned, flashing him a smile, gathering the wrapper about her, rising to drop him a little curtsy.

He bowed gracefully. "I've been admiring you so vocally that Lily grew tired of listening and brought me here to see you face to face," he told her with a smile.

"Flatterer," she scolded, reseating herself with a show of pale white thighs as the wrapper slid aside. "Please be seated, if you don't mind watching a woman primp a bit."

Bannerman laughed, well aware that his heart was hammering like that of a schoolboy. Up this close, Mrs. Creegan was even more intoxicating than seen from the other side of the footlamps. She was in her early thirties, he guessed, and her body was soft and rounded. She was not so much the paid stage performer as she was a neighborhood wife playing at theatricals. Shrewdly, he decided this must be the foundation on which her tremendous appeal was based.

"I told Lily tonight that within five years you'd both be wealthy women," he began, watching her fingertips tuck in a few wisps of stray black hair. "I like to feel I'm business-man enough to make a prophecy like that and know it will come true."

Her eyes and lips laughed at him. "You're a very danger-ous man, sir. You tell a woman things she wants to hear. Not about herself but about matters in which she is vitally interested."

"Does money mean so much to you?"

"Yes and no. I have a little girl. I've sworn she'll never have to do what—what I do to earn a living."

"You do it very well. So well that you interest an old sobersides like me in a manner in which no other woman—"

He broke off at sight of her upraised hand. "Mr. Banner-man, be good enough to forgive me for what I'm about to say. I'm a stage performer, but I'm no bought woman. I pick my friends not for their money, but for their personal qualifications. Do I make myself clear?"

His flush made him even more handsome, she reflected. Drawing a deep breath, he murmured, "It's my turn to apologize. I meant no offense, believe me." He came to his feet, tall and worldly in his impeccable Redfern garments. "May I at least beg the privilege of coming backstage from time to time to see you? Perhaps we can find some mutual interest on which to converse."

Her glance was friendly. "Such as profitable ventures in which to invest the great wealth you predict for me?"

His laughter was born of genuine amusement. *"Touche!* Profitable ventures it shall be. Nothing more personal— unless you yourself suggest it."

She held out her hand. Bannerman bent and kissed it.

As he shut the dressing room door behind him, the real estate titan decided that, in one way or another, Mike Gannon or no Mike Gannon, he was going to possess the beautiful woman he'd just met. If Gannon was stupid enough to interfere, it would be too bad for Michael Gannon.

Bannerman whistled as he walked jauntily toward the stage door.

CHAPTER SEVEN

An arm about her daughter, Moira Creegan entered the courtroom.

There was terror in her eyes and a wild thudding in her heart. Her legs were weak and her skin crawled. Every few moments her gloved hand would tighten, pressing Kathleen against her hip.

She was going to lose her child!

After all the years, after all the struggles with her pride and modesty, they would come and take her away. Everything she had built was being washed down the drain. She was accused of being a sinful woman, a strumpet unfit to raise a daughter. And because of this she hated Aunt Martha Creegan and Elvira Tomkins with a fierce and savage fury.

She had been right that evening last year in The Mummy Case, when she had seen young Morgan Davies in the audience. He had kept silent for a long time, but a slip of the tongue to the wrong person, the swiftness of malicious gossip—

"Your sisters-in-law are very determined about this thing," Frank Bannerman had told her in his office. "They mean to take Kathleen away from you, back to Rome. They claim —permit me to be brutal, my dear—that you're no better than a common woman."

"They can't, they can't," she had whispered in horror.

She had been too distrait to cry. She'd done enough of that the day before when a process server had found her at the Jennings boarding house and had served her with the legal papers which now lay across Bannerman's desk. Her first thought had been to turn to Mike.

"You're lucky they didn't serve you at The Golden Tassel," Mike had said bitterly when she sought him out. "This way, at least, you have a chance."

"What can I do, Mike? What?"

"Marry me. Then we can spit in their eyes together."

Yes. It was a way out, but not the way for Moira Creegan. Not until she had exhausted every other chance. There was always Frank Bannerman. Since the night she'd first met him, Moira had been hearing good things about him. A power in the city, he was respected and liked. In some quarters, he was even feared. He would know about lawsuits.

Bannerman's hand tapped a letter opener on the desk as his eyes touched her pale face. "You'll need more than a good lawyer. I've already contacted Brandon Partridge of Partridge, Heap and Taggart. One of the oldest and ablest legal firms in Buffalo. They handle all my work.

"But as I say, we need something more than that. A lawyer needs evidence with which to fight, just as a soldier needs a rifle and ammunition. Well! We've got to—ahem— manufacture some."

"I—I don't understand."

His lips curved into a smile. Moira Creegan was a beautiful woman. Her mouth was parted in her fear, but it was full and moist, indicative of passion. Frank Bannerman intended to sample that passion before very long. To him, this lawsuit was a godsend. He could not have asked for a better way in which to put her in his debt.

He cleared his throat. "If Morgan Davies testifies that he saw you doing that bathing suit act, you're finished."

"And he will testify, he will," she whimpered. "He's Phineas Davies' nephew. Nothing can possibly stop him."

"Well, now. I'm not so sure about that. Do you know where he is right now?"

Dumbly she stared at him, shaking her head. Bannerman laughed softly. "Neither does his uncle, nor any of his family. I know because I told him where to go. For your information he's on an extended fishing tour five hundred miles from Buffalo. Naturally, he couldn't afford to do that unless he were certain he had a good job waiting for him when he came back."

"A good job?" she echoed.

"Morgan Davies wants to practice corporation law. Partridge, Heap and Taggart specialize in just such practice. He walks into that firm as a junior partner—after the judge hands down his decision in your case."

"Oh! I—you're a miracle worker, Frank!"

His upraised hand held her silent. "I've done more than that. You've been telling Mrs. Jennings you travel a lot. I I own a number of dummy corporations. One of them is Western Developments. I've toyed with the idea of expanding into Cleveland and Detroit. I employed you to scout those territories for me, you understand? You do travel a lot. For Western Developments."

He opened a desk drawer and drew out a thick file crammed with papers. "This contains everything about the corporation and what you may need to know in case you're called to the stand. Partridge won't call you. The plaintiff's attorney might. I want you to be prepared.

"Naturally, you won't go back to The Golden Tassel until after judgment has been given. Not even to visit. You understand?"

"But men who've seen me—won't they—?"

"What men?" he asked with a smile. "Canawlers? Everybody knows you. Everybody loves you. Great Lakes sailors? You think they'd let the people from above The Terrace do anything to you? Besides, I've already passed word around. The man who takes the chair against you—"

He shook his head to hide the ugly look stamping lines on his face. He was so close to winning this woman that he'd cheerfully kill any man who stood in his way.

Now Moira Creegan was sitting tensely on the edge of a courtroom bench, listening to the lawyers arguing over an adjournment. The case had been put over four times already while Phineas Davies turned western New York State over in an unsuccessful hunt for his absent nephew. Brandon Partridge was objecting strenuously to a fifth adjournment, explaining that this constant harassment of his client was turning her into an ill woman.

The judge had read the complaint. He looked now at Moira Creegan and found himself unable to believe that this poised, respectable woman dressed so fashionably, could ever have removed her garments before a male audience. His scowl darkened as he turned toward a perspiring Phineas Davies.

"Motion for adjournment denied, counselor. I think we'd best resolve the matters at issue here and now, in fairness to everyone concerned."

Her hands were cleanched so tightly they ached, Moira realized as she watched and heard the parade of witnesses to the chair, but she could not have moved for the world. Half a dozen disreputable characters testified they had seen the bathing cart performance on the stage of The Mummy Case. Four of them could not identify the defendant as the entertainer who had held them spellbound. One witness grudgingly said it might be she, but on cross-examination

90

Brandon Partridge compelled him to admit he was not at all certain, that he'd had a seat in the rear of the hall, and that more than half the time men standing on chairs or tables had blocked his view.

Only one witness was adamant. He positively identified Moira Creegan as the entertainer. As he rose to cross-examine, Brandon Partridge was curious. He wanted to know why the witness was so positive.

"I just know, that's all. I know her," the man said flatly.

"Then you can tell us the color of the bathing cart," the lawyer said affably, "and describe the clothes the defendant is alleged to have removed."

"I wasn't looking at the bathin' cart."

"What about her clothes? How was she dressed?"

There was a little silence. The man had a squinting look to his eyes that made him seem lost and frightened. Moira almost felt sorry for him. He sat rigid in his chair, elbows on its arms and from time to time he wiped away the sweat beading his forehead. In answer to the question, he shook his head.

"Speak up," Partridge encouraged. "You shook your head. The answer to my question must be, you don't know. Is that correct?"

"Yes. I—don't know. I was lookin' at her face."

Brandon Partridge turned to his counsel table, lifted a sheet of printed matter and handed it to the witness. "Read that, please," he smiled.

The witness read it, loudly and firmly. Partridge took away the paper, then asked, "Where in the audience were you sitting on the night you claim to have seen the defendant on the stage of The Mummy Case?"

"Somewhere in the middle of the room. Fifty, sixty feet away."

"In other words, roughly the length of this judicial chamber, which is—I believe the Court will take judicial recognition of the fact—exactly fifty-seven feet, six inches long."

"About that," the man muttered.

Brandon Partridge turned to the judge. "I ask that the defendant be directed to walk out into the hall, Your Honor, then to return in a minute."

The judge looked over his pince-nez at Moira. Patting Kathleen on the shoulder, she rose to her feet and moved out past the leather-covered doors into the corridor. She stopped short, staring. Five women—each dressed exactly like her, with black hair done up in her own coiffure and carrying the same pocketbooks—stood waiting for her to join them.

"You walk with us, dearie," one of them smiled, moving aside so Moira might step into line. "Ready, girls?"

Even the judge gasped at sight of the six women. The witness stared dumbly, unable yet to understand his predicament. Brandon Partridge lifted a hand and the six women lined up against the far wall of the courtroom.

"Now, sir, pick out the defendant in the case."

The witness licked his lips. "I—my eyeglasses. . ."

"Eyeglasses? This is the first time we've heard anything about spectacles. If you need them so badly, why don't you have them on?"

Without waiting for a reply, Partridge continued, and now his voice grew harsh and menacing, "You've never owned a pair of spectacles, have you? Your name is Squinty Doland. You can see up to ten feet away. Beyond that you're as blind as a mole. Isn't that so, sir?"

"I—"

The judge looked down at the witness. "I want the truth. If you lie to me I'll see to it you face charges of perjury and contempt of court."

"No," the man mumbled. "I never had no eyeglasses."

"But you need them?" Partridge thundered.

"For more'n about ten feet, I do."

"On the night in question, you saw very little of what happened on The Mummy Case stage, is that correct?"

"I tried to get closer but there was so many men—"

"Step down," the judge said grimly. "I want this man remanded to the city jail and the district attorney instructed to arraign him for perjury. All right, counselor, let's get on with the rest of it."

At the close of the plaintiff's testimony, Brandon Partridge moved to dismiss on the ground that the plaintiffs had failed to make out a *prima facie* case. The judge took the motion under advisement. Brandon Partridge presented evidence that Moira Creegan had been working for Western Developments for the past three years, that she spent her days while in Buffalo at the Jennings boarding house. Bertha Jennings proved an excellent witness. She was indignant and did not hesitate to admit it.

"Little Kathleen goes to a private school. She attends Sunday church services with her mother when she's home, with my husband and me when Mrs. Creegan's got to be working. Anyone says Mrs. Creegan isn't a fit mother is a mean and spiteful liar."

The judge looked down at Aunt Martha Creegan and Elvira Tomkins over his pince-nez and cleared his throat. "I think I've heard enough testimony," he said drily, and reached for his notes. "I'll make my decision by the end of the week."

It was over. Instinctively, Moira knew she had won.

Her head bent and she began to weep, very softly.

Frank Bannerman pointed his finger at Black John Bennett.

"You'll have no more to do with Mike Gannon until I give the word, my friend. Let that fact be clearly understood between us. Let bygones be bygones."

Bennett squirmed in the big leather chair which held his heavy body. A big man on Canal Street, he felt small and insignificant in these rich offices where Frank Bannerman lorded it over his corner of the world. "When he makes trouble—" he began.

Bannerman chuckled. "When he makes trouble, we'll make trouble. But not before. I have certain—plans—which I mean to see carried to a proper conclusion." He would not explain to the uncomfortable Irishman that he meant the bedding of Moira Creegan, but his mind toyed with the thought of the handsome Mrs. Creegan stark naked in a hotel room with him.

"The further annoyance of Mike Gannon," he went on, "has no part in those plans. As a matter of strict fact, annoying him any longer might cause me embarrassment." By which he meant, If we make a martyr out of him we may rouse Moira Creegan's sympathy, which would be a tactical error. Making such errors was abhorrent to Frank Bannerman.

"All right," Bennett growled. "If that's the way you want it."

"Concentrate your energies on developing the Empire Line, John. You'll have plenty to keep you busy. And there's more than enough haulage on the Erie to make both Gannon and us fairly wealthy."

His attitude indicated that their conference was ended. Bennett reached for his gray derby, rose to his feet and left the office.

Bannerman's secretary came in to announce, "A young woman to see you, sir. She says her name is Lily Anders."

The Egyptian. And right on time. Bannerman leaned back in his chair. "Send her in, Miss Loomis. I am not to be disturbed under any circumstances."

He came to his feet as The Egyptian swept into the room with a swirl of her long taffeta skirt.

"Lily, you grow more lovely every hour."

She stared back at him coolly, disengaging her hand. "You didn't bring me here to tell me that. What's on your mind?"

The Egyptian was out of her element in a business office and was nervous. She took the chair he offered, her eyes moving to the oil paintings on the walls, to the glass cabinets lined with leather-bound books, then watched Bannerman move around the edge of his desk to seat himself. Above the tips of his fingers, which he pressed together to form a vee, his eyes regarded her. "Lily, I want you to do me a favor."

She started, eyeing him carefully. "What sort of favor?"

"I want you to make love to Mike Gannon."

The Egyptian opened her mouth, then closed it. She drew a deep breath. "I can't do it. It isn't that I object for personal reasons, you understand. He's good in bed, is Mike Gannon. No, it isn't that. It's the fact that he's sweet on Moira Creegan. Never touches anybody but her."

"Exactly. And Moira's been living at the Jennings boarding house ever since she was served with a summons. Close to a year now, isn't it? Gannon visits her upon occasion, I know. He takes her and Kathleen to the theater or out to dinner. But there's been no love-making between them, I've made sure. I've had them both watched."

"You're keen for her," the woman stated.

"I admit it. I mean to make her my mistress." He could lie to Black John Bennett but The Egyptian, being a woman, was another matter. He had the feeling that unfailing honesty might be his best policy.

Bannerman leaned elbows on his desk. "I want you to stage it just right. I want Moira to walk in when you're both in bed."

The woman gaped. "You're mad," she managed to say, and stood up. The determined manner in which she

94

straightened her gloves and the tightness of her mouth echoed her emotions.

"Everybody has a price, Lily. What's yours?"

She hesitated, looking sideways at him. "Nothing you'd pay."

"Try me."

"Part ownership of The Golden Tassel buildings."

He frowned, considering. The rental from the Canal Street properties brought him a handsome profit year after year. To divide that with The Egyptian would hurt, but it was a price he could afford to pay.

"When Moira finds us together," the woman said wryly, "she'll want to claw my eyes out. Maybe she'll even want to dissolve our partnership. I have to have some financial protection."

Bannerman put his hands palm down on his desk.

"You have a deal, Lily. Come back this time tomorrow. I'll have papers ready for you to sign."

"What about Moira? How can you be sure she'll walk in on us?"

"Judge Walker is signing the judgment this afternoon. It will be recorded on Monday. Soon after, I'll pay her a visit in my brougham. I'll bring her to The Tassel myself, when we're ready. Gannon isn't due back from Utica for another week."

"Just send me word. I'll be ready."

The Egyptian smiled faintly, alive with anticipation.

The days went slowly for Moira Creegan. She was anxious to be back at The Golden Tassel, yet she was well aware that her enforced imprisonment at the Jennings boarding house afforded her an unexpected opportunity to get to know Kathleen as an individual. Until now, though everything she did was directed toward making Kathy's life happier and more secure than her own, she had spent so little time with her, she seemed almost a stranger.

Now, however, they were always together in the mornings. And in the afternoons there were visits to be made together to the Washington Market for shopping, to the Genessee Street Bridge to look at the canal boat colony moored to the long wooden docks, and sometimes, even to the Music Hall.

Mike Gannon was away on one of his interminably long hauls. Since the trial, he had paid them a flying visit, to take them both to the Casino Theatre. Kathleen, now in her eleventh year, was growing swiftly and Mike teased Moira, saying that if she didn't hurry up and marry him, he'd ask her daughter. He always made his joking threat with a smile but if Moira was looking into his eyes at the time, she could see the longing and the hurt deep inside him.

Frank Bannerman was even more of a companion than Mike Gannon. Suave and polished, always impeccably attired, he paid Moira court with flowers and large boxes of candy. They ate out twice a week, at least, at the Niagara Hotel.

On a warm evening in late June a glittering black brougham drew up before the Jennings boarding house. Bannerman bowed to Moira, kissing her fingertips.

"Tonight you go back to The Golden Tassel, *ma belle amoureuse.*" He smiled. "But only after the theater and a late supper of oysters and champagne at my club."

One thing she had to say for Frank Bannerman, Moira reflected as she went down the porch steps with a hand resting on his forearm: he always did things in the grand style.

Mike Gannon was angry at himself.

He paced the thick Turkish carpet of the rooms above The Golden Tassel, driving a big fist into his palm, muttering oaths between his teeth. Fool! Fool! Not to have checked before coming to The Golden Tassel at such a late hour! Moira had not yet moved back from her lodgings at Jennings boarding house. He had been positive that he would find her here, flushed and triumphant from her stage show, ready to fall into his arms. Ever since the service of the summons in the action to have her declared an unfit mother, he'd seen precious little of Moira Creegan.

A footfall swung him toward the opening door.

He took a step forward, then stopped. The Egyptian was entering the room, showing surprise at sight of him. A thin wrapper appeared to be all she wore, though he caught sight of a shapely leg in a black silk stocking when the wrapper fell away to her stride.

"Oh! I thought Moira'd come back. I heard you talking."

"To myself. Where is she?"

"Still at Jennings', I guess."

She came across the room to the wall mirror, lifting her arms to fluff at her hair. The thin sleeves fell back, revealing smooth arms. Her heavy breasts lifted to punch thrusting nipples against the wrapper. Staring frankly, Mike Gannon began to remember that night so long ago when he and this woman had shared several hours of love-making. He moved about the room, suddenly uncomfortable, but he could not avoid the musky perfume in which she was misted.

Lily turned and smiled at him, reaching to the silver box. Putting a cigarette between her lips, she waited while he approached and struck a match.

"She may not be back for a long time. Frank Bannerman's been advising her, you know."

Mike groaned. "He helped her when I couldn't."

The Egyptian moved with swinging haunches toward the Belter sofa, throwing herself into it with both arms stretched across its back. She crossed her legs casually, ignoring the fact that a fold of the wrapper fell aside to show her heavy thigh from hip to knee.

"Sit down," she invited, waving the hand in which she held the cigarette. "Light up a cigar. Make yourself comfortable. Moira won't be here. The Tassel's closed. Enjoy yourself."

Later, he never remembered what it was they talked of, with The Egyptian sprawled in the sofa and with him seated across from her in a leather-covered Morris chair. From time to time she would remember that the front of her wrapper was loose, that it gaped to expose the inner swells of her breasts, and clutch it to her with a hand; but always as she did so, her eyes touched Mike slyly and with hunger.

It became a game to them.

The woman crossed her legs to expose her left leg. She bent forward, snubbing out her cigarette in a ceramic ash tray, knowing that one entire breast swung naked to his stare. Mike fought the desire she was breeding in him, trying to keep Moira in the forefront of his mind.

How far would she have to go to get the big canawler out of the Morris chair? Lily wondered. Throw off the wrapper and sit naked to her navel with her hard breasts jutting straight at him? Or cross her legs some more, letting him see that all she had on were the black silk stockings fastened with red garters and the high-heeled shoes?

She slid from the couch to go to the silver cigarette box again, but she had taken only two steps when Mike was off the Morris chair, arms going around her, lifting her off her feet, hands sliding up the backs of her stockinged legs to her naked thighs. She gasped at his strength and at the hunger for her flesh.

"Mike! Let go of—"

"Let you go, is it? And me with all this need for you? And you with your breasts so full and hard, your hips so eager?"

"We shouldn't—"

She felt she had to make the protest so as not to arouse his suspicions. But his mouth, moving across her soft throat and to the slopes of her soft bosom, left her with no will to think. All that was alive in her body was a feverish hunger for this man. She wanted to urge him to hurry, hurry! They had to be in bed when Moira and Frank Bannerman came walking through the door.

Ah, but what woman could hurry such a man?

He was gentle and tender, with an air of suppressed savagery about him, as though he restrained the fiery desperation of his body only for her sake. As she had teased him, so now he teased her, with lips and fingers.

Lily uttered soft cries as she felt the tide of sensation running free and wild within the confines of her flesh, thudding and pulsing, needing liberation, desperate for release and freedom.

Then the floor rocked under her bare feet and she stood swaying, watching him throw his clothes recklessly about the room. Now his hands were yanking at her wrapper, freeing her of its sash and sleeves.

She reached for him but he held her off, turning her with his hands and sitting in the Morris chair, then drawing her down on him. The Egyptian cried out thickly. The muscles of her thighs tensed and bunched. She began to curse slowly and monotonously, as their bodies joined in a taut, frenzied rhythm of motion.

Delirium was an eternity of sensual impressions, the scratch of ragged breathing and the distant ticking of a clock. Life flowed on in a thick river of delight, punctuated by whispers and soft kisses, the brush of hands on satin-smooth skin. . . .

The scream came from the open doorway, where Moira Creegan stood with a hand lifted to her open mouth and her eyes wide with disbelief and horror. A fur muff dangled from her wrist. She was smartly dressed in a fashionable green satin Polonaise gown, fitted with curtain drapery and

98

a waterfall back, with a matching pelerine thrown about her shoulders. Her eyes grew wide and stormy. For an instant she seemed poised to flee, then her chin lifted and she stepped swiftly across the thick rug.

The Egyptian was away from Mike Gannon, her hand outstretched for her wrapper, when Moira slammed into her. Curving fingers went into the loosened brown hair which spilled about the naked woman's shoulders and tugged savagely. Crying out with pain, Lily Anders whirled and slammed a hand against Moira's face.

Then they were clawing and scratching, crying out in a black, bitter anger. They went off their feet in a melee of naked legs and ripping green satin. They rolled over and over across the carpet, fingernails clawing, teeth bared and biting.

Mike was standing with one trouser leg on and one off as they careened into his ankles, taking his feet out from under him. He went down hard just as Moira aimed a palm straight for his cheek.

She screamed, "I'll kill you for this, Michael Gannon!"

Then The Egyptian sank her teeth in a bared shoulder and Moira erupted in fury, sobbing and cursing wildly, her hands balled into fists which she pummeled into the soft belly of the naked woman. Each tore at the other's hair. Each bit down hard at exposed flesh. Lily had ripped the Polonaise dress from bodice to hip, revealing the lace camisole beneath.

Frank Bannerman stood framed in the doorway, stunned by the unexpected violence. He had expected Moira Creegan to turn from the sight of her lover enjoying himself with her business partner, and to weep on his shoulder. His position would have been secure, then; he could have offered her consolation; he had been positive that, as a woman scorned, she would have fallen into his arms.

He ran forward to separate them and took a high-heeled shoe in his groin, bending him double with pain. His gray derby toppled to the floor. The Egyptian rolled over it with Moira, straddling her hips, slapping hard at her flushed face.

"Look," groaned Bannerman. "Here, now. You can't—"

Mike Gannon elbowed him aside. "You've had no experience with fighting females, sir. Let me show you the technique."

The big Irishman had donned his trousers. Below and

99

above them he was naked. His big hands went out and his fingers twisted in thick brown hair and disarranged black hair. He gave a tug, another yank, and then a solid jerk. Both women screamed in pain but they came apart. With his fingers in their hair he held them at arms' length.

"It's ashamed of yourselves you ought to be," he growled.

"Ash—ashamed?" Moira screeched. "I'll claw your eyes out!" She tried to reach him but his grip was too tight.

"Lily, go put your wrapper on," Mike ordered, releasing her.

For a moment she looked as if she might hurl herself on Moira again, but she shrugged, touched her breasts gingerly, looked down at the bruises on her belly and thighs, and glowered darkly at Bannerman. She opened her mouth as if to speak, then closed it, lifting her wrapper and shrugging into it. She walked out of the room with head held high.

"All right, Michael Gannon. All right! You can let go of me now," snapped Moira.

"I'm not so sure, mavourneen. You have the devil in your eyes."

"You black-hearted gossoon. Oh, Mike—you *bastard!*"

He let her go without a word. Bending, he lifted his thrown clothes from the back of the Belter sofa, from a lampshade, from the floor. A flush rode his cheeks and he could not look at the woman who was vainly trying to put herself to rights with clasps and pins.

"I—I'll dress outside in the hall," he muttered.

Frank Bannerman waited until the door closed behind him. "Moira, I don't know what to say."

"Don't say anything then," she hinted darkly.

Tears glistened in her eyes. A moment more and they would be spilling over, flooding her cheeks. She did not want Frank Bannerman to see her heartbreak, her inconsolable despair. This man had been good to her in his fashion. He deserved more from Moira Creegan than quivering lips and running eyes.

"Of course I understand." He had caught the finality in her tones. For one black moment he thought that his expensive plan had failed. The woman would taken Gannon back to her bed; she would forgive, even if she might not forget, his faithlessness.

Moira brushed at her tears with the heel of a palm, then swung around smiling and bright. "I'm sorry. I didn't mean to snap. The shock—"

"Don't say another thing. I only regret it happened. If I may do anything to help . . ."

"Not now, Frank. Please be patient just a little longer. I want to see you soon, here in my rooms. A small supper, just the two of us?"

He made a little bow to conceal his elation. An intimate *tête-à-tête*, just the two of them, with chilled oysters and grilled steak, with iced champagne. Yes. In such a setting, he would be paid back for what this dismal night was costing him.

Moira Creegan and The Egyptian met three weeks later in the plush offices of Partridge, Heap and Taggart. Neither would look at the other, and they conducted their conversation through their attorneys.

"Tell the woman I'm asking a hundred thousand dollars in cash for my interest in The Golden Tassel," said Lily Anders to her lawyer, Bellamy Moulton.

"You," Moira snapped at Brandon Partridge, "tell that—that creature the business isn't worth twenty."

"Naturally, without me to run things—"

"You? Run things? Why, you painted—"

"Ladies," said Brandon Partridge firmly.

"Please," begged Bellamy Moulton.

The Egyptian said loftily, "I'll sign for seventy-five thousand."

"Not a cent more than fifty!"

The lawyers talked for a while, comparing ledgers, seeking to find a talking point. Moira stared out the window. For the life of her, she would not look at this woman; to do so would bring back the memory of her with Mike on that Morris chair. And if she thought of *that* again, she would go mad.

She had neither seen nor heard from the big Irishman since that night. She and Lily, via a series of notes carried back and forth between them by one of the charwomen, had assured one another that the continuance of their partnership was no longer possible. The sooner one bought out the other, the sooner each would be content.

Moira offered to do the buying. She found Lily oddly agreeable.

All that remained was to establish a price, to get it down on legal cap and to attach their signatures.

Moira said suddenly, "Sixty thousand for The Golden

101

Tassel, lock, stock and barrel. No more, no less. What about it, Lily?"

Lily said flatly, "It's a deal. I'll be at the Niagara Hotel, Mr. Moulton. When you have the papers ready, notify me."

She went out with a swagger to her hips, parasol tapping the rug at every stride. Moira stared down at her pointed shoes. Sixty thousand dollars was a lot of money. She would have to raise a mortgage, she supposed.

Frank Bannerman might help her there.

CHAPTER EIGHT

Silver candelabra made the crystalware glisten as if filled with rainbow colors in the parlor of her suite. The console table had been spread with a white tablecloth and set for a dinner à *deux*. In the hall, the caterer had set up his serving tables. It was five minutes to nine o'clock on the first Saturday of August.

Moira Creegan sat at her vanity bench staring at her reflection in the triple mirrors. A gown of apricot velvet, low-cut to show smooth white shoulders and the upper swells of her bosom, clung to her tightly at waist and hips. When she moved, the velvet caught light from the gas lamps and candles and appeared to gleam. A pearl choker about her throat, a pearl bracelet and a single large pearl ring gave her an aura of elegance.

Just this way might she have dressed for a fashionable dinner party back in Rome at the Creegan house on Depeyster Street. In one sense she found it more exciting to be so dressed, rather than to be wearing a thin linen wrapper, the way Lily had with Mike in this same suite of rooms. If Frank Bannerman wanted her, he would have to make a play for her. She was a little too proud to tumble into his arms like a streetwalker.

When she heard the hall door open into the parlor she rose and left the bedroom, walking with her left hand holding the sweeping velvet skirt, her right hand outstretched. "Frank! So good of you to come."

He kissed the palm of her hand, smiling faintly. "Moira, Moira. You must be jesting. Haven't you understood at all how very much I've looked forward to this night for the past two years? Wild horses couldn't have kept me away."

"You flatter me, dear." She turned and rather breathlessly indicated the magnum of champagne in the ice bucket, but the society man was not so easily dismissed.

He came up behind her, pressing close, his arms about her middle and his lips on her bared shoulder. "How very much I've needed this night. How very, very much. And at the moment I find myself extremely selfish. I'm not even going to ask how you feel. Pleasant enough for me is the fact I'm here with you in my arms."

Moira admitted that the arms banding her middle were not unexciting. She had not been near a man since the long-ago service of the summons in her court action; perhaps this was the reason why her breasts filled out hard and swollen when she felt his strength against her.

She turned, whether to speak or not she never clearly knew. His mouth was there waiting and at its touch her own mouth loosened and went slack, then was mashed flat before the fury of his kiss. She moaned a little as his hand slid around behind her hips to urge her against him. His tongue came thrusting and, as if it possessed a will of its own, her own stabbed out to meet it. They clung together for many moments before his arms released her.

"I think I'm dreaming," he whispered, kissing the tip of her nose. "I've had dreams like this before, you know. And always at a certain point, they faded out and I woke up in an empty bed."

She could not stop the slamming of her heart nor still the trembling of her legs. She half laughed, leaning her soft belly to him. "Tell me when your dream would stop, darling. I'll see if I can put a proper ending to it."

"Moira, Moira!" he cried, bringing her against him again, raking his lips across her shoulders and down to the exposed flesh of her breasts above the apricot velvet bodice. "I adore you. I worship you. There's never been another woman like you. Not Cleopatra or Delilah or Venus herself."

Her fingertips traced his lips. "You say such nice things. What else would these lips say if I filled you with champagne?"

"Try me," he laughed, and released her.

They sipped the golden liquor by candlelight, close together on the Belter sofa. Moira Creegan had never been

103

more provocative, Bannerman told himself. An aura of perfume drifted about her shoulders. Her laughter, as it rang out, was husky, sensual. And her eyes! Ah, her eyes were feverish and promising.

Conversation neither speeded nor lagged between them. They spoke of the fire which had destroyed the Hotel Richmond, of the commission which had been recently appointed to report on a possible State barge canal. Work projects were promised on the canals, to deepen the Erie and Oswego waterways to a depth of nine feet. All this and other things they chatted over, with a sense of timelessness which neither slowed nor hurried their speech.

They ate the steak and salad, still in that same mood of inevitability. Moira felt the champagne working in her veins like some strange opium of the spirit, heightening her sense of floating in a vacuum. Beneath her gown her thighs were pressed close together. In mock symbolism of a lost virginity? Only two men in all her life had known the secrets of her woman's flesh—her dead husband Richard, and Mike Gannon. Now a third man was soon to know her intimately.

She had no need to be reticent. Right now she wanted Frank Bannerman to know the hidden beauty of her body. Lazily she wanted to sprawl out before him temptingly, drive him mad with glimpses of her flesh, with the erotic wisdom she had gained in a lifetime. There would be no fight in her. If anything, she would do all she could to please this man.

Her full red mouth quirked in a languid smile. She pushed her chair back and rose to her feet, coming around the corner of the little table. Impish delight bubbled in her as she saw the pleased surprise come to life in his eyes as she sat across his thighs.

She tilted his head back and pressed her open lips to his mouth. Her soft thighs wriggled gently as she squirmed closer, so that he might know the full magnificence of her breasts. Ah! Now he was responding to her. Fully alive, his breath was scratching in his throat and his palms were sliding down her back and across her hips.

Her teeth nipped his earlobe, then his throat. Breathing warmth against him, without speaking. Stir him, rouse him! Yes. Like this, groaning and trying to get her velvet gown down off her shoulders, face flushed red and eyes oddly

104

glazed. Seeing him so helpless before her teasings filled Moira Creegan with a sense of power.

She laughed and was halfway across the room before Frank Bannerman could bring his gaze to focus. He stood up, big and strong in his immaculately tailored evening clothes. On silent feet he came across the thick Turkish carpet.

She tried to run but he was too close behind her. His arms went under her armpits and to the front of the apricot dress. "Frank," she whispered, looking down at the fingers busily engaged in gripping the material firmly. "It's a brand new dress."

The sound of the seams parting scratched at their nerves. Moira felt a little of the pressure against her swollen breasts give way as they surged upward into the black lace of her undergarment. Black lace on smooth white flesh, with the nipples proudly erect; only for an instant did she see them before his hands came up to cover, to hold them gently.

"This is a part of my dream, my dear."

"Is it, Frank?"

"Ah, yes. And this, too. Gently—oh, so very gently I draw down the lace until you are all out in the open in the candlelight."

"You have such wonderful dreams, darling."

"This is only the beginning," he breathed.

The tumult of sensation within her body was at full flood now. His hands and then his lips were teaching her a madness which she had shared only with Mike Gannon in the past.

Mike? Oh damn him all to hell!

He and Lily in the chair. She closed her eyes and turned her face to rest her cheek against Bannerman's shirt front. Some of the eagerness had gone out of her, she realized, and she squeezed her eyes shut to fight the tears that threatened to come storming past her eyelids. If only it were her big Irishman here, pleasing her this way! But she had lost Mike Gannon forever. He had hurt her too deeply. Filled with her sense of loss, she understood suddenly that her pride had been injured; and because of that injured pride, she felt the need to establish herself as a desirable woman in her own mind.

"Do you like me like this, Frank?" she whispered.

"Can't you tell?"

"Yes. Yes, I can. But I want it in more than words, in more than just a saying so. I want—"

What did she want? Her head shook helplessly back and forth. Savagely she refused the insistent thought that even as Frank Bannerman caressed her breasts, she wanted Mike Gannon.

Damn you, Mike. Ah, damn you!

She cursed softly, tears filling her eyes. Bannerman, noting how disturbed she was, thought it was because of his searching, stroking hands and gently caressing lips. Elation rose within him. She was finally showing the passion of which she was capable.

To further rouse that desire, he drew her down beside him on the Belter sofa and now his hands were sliding under the long velvet skirt and up the stockinged legs to her naked thighs, stroking them with wanton insistence.

"Don't tease me any more," she whimpered.

"This is all a part of my dream, darling. You remember I told you about it?"

"Yes, but—"

His head bent and his lips searched her soft flesh.

Her hands caught his head and held it still. With eyes wide open she stared upward at the blank white ceiling. "Frank, I never realized a man like you could have so much hunger for a woman."

"Don't you like that hunger?"

"Yes! Oh, yes."

He said no more words but his hands and his lips were adding to the fire in her flesh, and she cried out softly and then more harshly as the flames of that fire grew and grew within her. The apricot velvet dress was rumpled in torn strips beneath her. The black lace undergarments were shredded, peeled back on either side.

There was no more protest in her, for she had made up her mind that she would belong to this man ever since the night—forget Mike! Forget him and Lily! Enjoy this moment as Mike had enjoyed those moments in the Morris chair!

She reached out and drew him to her and let him bring an ecstasy of forgetfulness into her mind and her body. *Drive out Mike Gannon,* her mind screamed at him. *Purge him from my senses. Let me belong to you, utterly and without*

106

thought. Make me yours, Frank Bannerman! With this rocking, writhing craziness, buy me forever.

As your woman.

Your mistress.

The Golden Tassel went right on doing business as usual when The Egyptian left. She walked out on an early afternoon, her chin held high, taffeta umbrella-skirt rustling to her every step, half a dozen porters carrying her trunks and bulging valises. Moira stood at a window of her parlor and watched her step into the waiting gig which would take her to the Lehigh Valley depot, already planning the entertainment for the evening.

Emotions were mixed in Moira Creegan. Nine years ago she had walked into this building an unknown, without a job. Penniless. Now she was sole owner. True, there was a big mortgage on it, but Frank Bannerman had waved a hand and told her to forget it.

Yet she would not forget it. She would pay it off as swiftly as she could. She let the curtain fall and turned away from the gig bearing The Egyptian out of her life. Her hand went to the bellpull.

"Send Penelope to me, Tansy," she told her maid.

Penelope Drayman was a new girl, eager and alert for money. Born in a boarding house just off The Terrace, she had come early to understand that a man would pay money to enjoy the embraces of an attractive woman; and Penny was attractive. Short and slim, but with a firm, large bosom and shapely legs, she had wandered into The Golden Tassel two days after its opening night, hunting a job.

Moira had taken an immediate liking to her. Nor, in the days that followed, had she seen fit to change her mind. Penny liked money as much as she did herself, and was always coming to her with ideas on how to enlarge the scope of her operations. A suggestion Penny had made some weeks before had remained in her mind. When she lay sleepless at night, Moira turned it over mentally, developing and enlarging upon it.

A footfall swung her toward the door. Penny came in smiling, gesturing at the window. "She's pulled stakes at last. You're the boss now."

Moira smiled faintly. "Then you're boss number two,

107

honey. I need somebody to help me run this place. I think you'd be a good choice. Naturally, you'll get a big increase in salary."

"You really mean it?" the shorter girl squealed. Then her face darkened. "If it means an office job, I don't want it. I'd die if I couldn't get out on that stage and—"

"I still perform, don't I? And I run the whole shebang. No, you can perform as much as you want. If you'd like a special number to star you, dream one up and we'll talk it over. Fair enough?"

"More than fair, Moira."

"Good, it's settled. I wanted to see you about something else, though. A couple of weeks ago you suggested fixing up some private rooms upstairs where a small group of rich men might enjoy themselves in privacy."

"You like the idea, then?"

"Mmmm, of course. But I have an even better plan. We'll have your private rooms, all right, but we'll add a larger room, a sort of replica of the big room downstairs. We have plenty of space, now that Lily's gone. A private club for special members, at a thousand dollars a year dues."

Penny pursed her red mouth and her eyes grew wide. "You'll make a fortune!"

"Isn't that what we want?" Moira wondered.

To be not only a mistress for Frank Bannerman but a rich mistress. Is this your goal in life, Moira Creegan? No, not quite. All she had done, she did with her daughter in mind, that she might not have to walk in her life the same steps Moira had walked in hers.

She sighed and looked at Penny. "How's Pam and her boy friend? They still as much in love as ever?"

Penny said, "She's a stupid fool. I tell her, but she won't listen. Her Kenneth this, her Kenneth that. Doesn't the simpleton know 'her Kenneth' is from Chippewa Street and will marry a girl from his own class, not a—"

"Go ahead, Penny. Say it. Not a whore. They say the truth hurts. You don't starve to death from the truth, nor die of thirst."

Penny said, as if to cheer her, "Well, at least Dotty's going to get married. She's been sporting an engagement ring this past week."

"No! Tell me all about it. Here, sit down."

She took an intense interest in her girls, suffering with

108

them when love appeared to turn its back on them, rejoicing when they were happy.

Dottie Alford was a farm girl, big and blond and buxom, who had wandered into Canal Street five years before. An unhappy love affair, a baby born to her and sold by her to a childless married woman for ten dollars in Utica, brought her into Canal Street hunting a job. Moira always felt a sort of kinship with her because of that fact, remembering the days of her own disappointments while job-hunting here in Buffalo.

Lately, Dottie had met a young canawler who owned his own barge. They were young and lonely, and Moira often had seen them sitting at a table just staring into each other's eyes and holding hands.

"Now Bill wants to marry her. Dottie says yes but she doesn't want him on the canal any longer. Says she wants him to be a farmer with her. Bill, he wants to buy a canal boat and start his own line."

"And?"

Penny smiled. "They're both being pretty stubborn. Who knows which'll win out? Then there's that young copper who comes to the back door nights, asking for a date with any girl who'll go out with him. He walks them up and down the street. Never touches the girls, just talks to them."

"Isn't that odd?"

"Not half so odd as what he asks each and every one of them. I've talked to all our girls who've gone out with him. Olive, Hortense, Betsey, Prue. They all report the same thing. Sometime during their walk he wants to know if they've ever seen a striped cow."

"A striped cow?" exclaimed Moira.

Penny nodded. "Umm-hmmmm. None of the girls laugh at him though. He's kind of sad about it, they tell me."

"But what in the world—why's he want to know that?"

"Nobody knows, and he won't tell."

"Send him in to see me, next time he comes. Maybe I can worm his secret out of him."

"All right, consider it done. Anything else?"

Moira waved her away. She wanted time to think, alone and by herself. There were details about her private club which she needed to work out. As she went over them mentally, she found her thoughts distracted by the problems facing Pam Ulrich and Dottie Alford. Oh, yes.

109

And the policeman who asked about a striped cow.

The days fled into weeks and, slowly, the dream of a private club on the upper floor of The Golden Tassel took on three dimensions. Carpenters and plumbers were once again at work, and when they were done, Moira brought Frank Bannerman to inspect their work.

A round dais covered with black velvet in the middle of the room caught the eye at once. Above it a chandelier was hung so that it beamed a solid circle of light all around the upraised stage. Tables and chairs—thirty in all—were so arranged that every diner would have a perfect view of what happened on the stage. Narrow strips of black velvet radiated outward from the dais like spokes from a wheel. Down these strips would come the waitresses and the entertainers.

"My God, woman," enthused Bannerman. "This is fabulous!"

"You really like it, Frank? You aren't just saying that to please me? I'd appreciate your honesty. I really would. This is business."

His arms hugged her slim middle. "A thousand dollars a year," he muttered. "Thirty tables, thirty thousand dollars. Just for the privilege of reserving four chairs at a table in an upstairs room of a Canal Street saloon."

Moira eyed him from under long, sooty lashes. "In two years I'll be able to pay off your mortgage. Will I get the business I need?"

Bannerman chuckled. "I'll name you ten men, not counting myself, who'll put signed checks in your hands on my say-so. And I'll say it for you, honey. I'll spread the word."

"Your friends will get their money's worth," she told him meaningfully. "I won't cheat them. Just make sure they're all healthy when they step inside this place. I don't want anyone keeling over with a heart attack once the show begins."

A thought made the society man turn, eyebrows lifted. "You aren't going to perform?"

"Certainly not. And I'm retiring from the stage downstairs. I've found a replacement who'll make the boys forget me. Penny. You know her."

"I'm going to tell you something, Moira. I'm glad as hell you've made this decision."

"You don't want me showing your friends in public what they know you enjoy in private."

He cleared his throat. "Something like that."

Moira smiled and patted his hand.

Two days later when she went looking for Penny to tell her that the costume sketches were ready for the seamstresses, Moira walked into a room the Drayman girl shared with redheaded Pamela Travis. The doorknob turned in her hand and she was three feet inside the little bedroom before she saw what was hanging by a rope from the gas fixture.

Moira whimpered, "Oh, no. Oh God—*no!*" Then she screamed.

Tansy came running, crying out, "What's the matter, Miz Creegan?"

Then she, too, began to screech, trying to cover her bulging eyes with trembling fingers. Neither woman could look away from the redhead Pamela Travis, with her neck twisted grotesquely and the thin rope cutting into the soft neck.

Penny came racing along the hall with Patty Dee at her heels. Penny gave one horrified look at her roommate, then grabbed Moira and a shaking, sobbing Tansy and dragged them out into the corridor.

"Get Doc Brenner," she snapped at a white-faced Patty. "For Moira, not for—for Pam. Nobody can do anything for her. I'll have to send somebody to the Delaware Avenue police station. Come on, Patty. Look alive!"

The police found a note written in a childish scrawl.

Tell Kenath I won't make any trouble for him like he is scared of becas this is my weddin presend to him.
Pam

Moira lay sleepless all night, unable to drive away the sight of the wry neck and bloated face and bulging eyes of the dead girl. Why? Why? she asked herself over and over again. Why for a man? Any man? There was always another when you lost one. After Richard there was Mike, and after Mike, Frank.

And after Frank?

No, no more men after Bannerman. She was no longer the

111

innocent who'd walked up the stairs of The Mummy Case and stood before The Egyptian asking for a job. She had money in the bank. She would have a lot more money after the next ten years. She wouldn't need anyone when that happened. Only Kathleen.

She would always need her daughter. Without her, there would be no goal in life, no reason for staying alive. It was that simple.

Officer Benjamin O'Hare had never seen Patty Dee before this night. He looked twice at her, hard, wondering if she might be the girl he had been hunting through the long years. He straightened as she walked past him in the corridor just off The Golden Tassel stage, lifting his police hat and making a little bow.

"Good evening, ma'am."

"Oh. You're the patrolman assigned here. I've heard about you," Patty smiled. He was tall and young and handsome in a craggy sort of way. His hair was black, his eyes blue, and there was the trace of a mustache growing on his upper lip. He seemed as friendly as a puppy.

"I was wondering, ma'am, if we might take a little stroll after—after the show's over. Just the two of us."

Patty considered, head tilted to one side. A stroll? Well, why not? There was nothing else to do down here on Canal Street, unless you took a young man to your room. And Mrs. Creegan did not exactly approve of such carryings-on. Of course, if you were careful about it and didn't flaunt your man around in front of everybody, she guessed it was all right. After all, everybody knew Mrs. Creegan entertained that rich society man in her parlor—and bedroom, too—three times a week.

It was done with such good manners, though. Nobody got screaming drunk or ran out into the corridor without a stitch on, the way Pam—Lord rest her soul!—had done once when her Kenneth was visiting her. No more young men would come to see Pamela Travis. Patty felt like crying.

"All right," she said slowly. "I'll go for a stroll. Not far, though. Mrs. Creegan wouldn't like it. Just a little ways."

"Naturally," he said stiffly, and looked indignant.

At the supper table, Patty mentioned her date to Penny Draymen. The older girl said, "Mrs. Creegan wants to see any girl officer O'Hare invites out. When you finish eating, we'll go see her together."

112

An hour later, sitting at the console table where she was eating a small repast of boiled ham and baked potato, Moira Creegan explained herself. She sat with legs crossed, her face grave, a look of haunted worry in her eyes.

"I don't know this young policeman, honey. He may be some sort of sex maniac, with this striped cow—whatever it may be—to trigger off his aberrations. I try to look after my girls. I don't want another tragedy like the one we had with Pam Travis.

"Oh, no," exclaimed Patty. "Oh, my, no."

As she walked with the patrolman through the dimly lighted streets, Patty told herself that Mrs. Creegan had no need to fret about young O'Hare. He was polite and soft-spoken, though big and rugged. Drunks looked at her and opened their mouths to make comments; then they looked at her companion and closed them. It was almost funny, she thought.

Not until they were standing close to the outer stairs in the backstage alley did he mention the striped cow. "Did you ever see one? Or connect it with anything?" he wanted to know. His eyes were sober, very serious. Though she wanted to giggle, she did not.

Patty shook her head. "I'm afraid not. I never did much traveling around the country. I was never a farm girl."

"The cow wasn't alive," he said as if to himself.

Patty put her hand on the banister rail and ran lightly up the stairs. At the landing she leaned over and smiled at him. "I never saw a striped cow but I had one once that was spotted like a leopard. It was stuffed full of cotton and I called it Boofy!"

"Boofy!" O'Hare said softly. "Oh, my God—yes! That's the name. I've tried so long to remember."

He looked absolutely insane, his eyes wild, face as pale as a new petticoat. Patty shrank back, seeing him come up the staircase, two treads at a time.

"Whats the matter? What is it?"

"Are you sure it was spotted? Not striped?"

She stared at him. "Of course I'm sure. I thought it was beautiful but the nearest I could come to it was 'boofy'. I—"

"Oh my God. *Angela!*"

Angela. Little angel. So long since anyone had called her that, not since she was a very tiny girl, before the big fire and—

113

"How did you know my name?" she whispered.

"I'm Ji! Your brother—you used to call me Ji, remember? You were only three years old. All I could recall about you was the stuffed cow. I thought it was striped."

The story came out in a spate of words from Benjamin O'Hare and a flood of tears from Angela. They had been five and three years old when the fire claimed their parents. A neighbor had saved them because they slept on the first floor. An uncle had taken Benjamin, but he had never been able to find out what happened to Angela.

"I lived with a neighbor. I can't tell you why she never gave me to Uncle Theodore. She brought me up. When I was twelve, she died penniless. I got a job on Canal Street. I was pretty. I got money to sing before men and do a dance. . ."

Her voice trailed off, remembering the way she had danced with so very little on, and the mustachioed man who had owned the saloon, who had taken her into his office and locked the door and removed her tights and raped her. She had been so ashamed; not because of what the man had done, but of her own reaction to it. She had enjoyed it. She had left the man and gone into The Mummy Case and a job in the chorus line.

Benjamin O'Hare put his hand over her mouth. "Don't tell me anything more," he pleaded. We're going to build a new life for you, sis."

"Oh, I couldn't leave Mrs. Creegan. She's counting on—"

She thought of her part in the stage show Moira was arranging for the Upstairs Club, and flushed. Shame made her tingle. She whispered, head hanging, "You'd better go. Forget me, Ji. I—"

O'Hare turned and pounded on the door, with Patty clinging to his arm begging him to be silent. He pummeled and kicked the panels until the burly caretaker came and let him in. He demanded to see Moira Creegan at once.

Moira had been working late in her parlor, but she gathered her satin wrapper closer and made room for them on her Belter sofa. She listened quietly, then smiled radiantly.

"Of course you can have her, Benjie. Take her away this night. Patty, you go pack your things. At once, do you understand? That's an order."

Patty was poised between tears and laughter, but she was too long used to obeying this handsome woman whose black hair was so faintly streaked with gray to disobey now. She stood and dropped a curtsy, then ran out.

Moira went across the room to her safe, opened it and lifted out a packet of hundred-dollar bills. She counted off five of them and gave them to the policeman. "For her dowry, Benjie. But she isn't to know. Not ever. Will you promise me that?"

He nodded dumbly, staring at the small fortune in his fingers.

Long after they had gone, Moira Creegan stared into the shadows of her upstairs parlor. Tears welled up in her eyes and ran down her cheeks. Why was there no brother Benjamin in her life, to come like a conquering angel and take *her* away from Canal Street?

The Upstairs Club opened on a cool December evening.

Candlelight, black velvet and haunting music throughout the room from unseen musicians, gave the diners a feeling of unreality. Pretty waitresses in high-heeled button shoes and black silk stockings and a frilly black lace apron—but otherwise unclothed—moved here and there between the tables carrying wine and champagne, Havana cigars, and club sandwiches. Smoke made a haze in the air, almost veiling the performer on the upraised black velvet stage.

Her name was Zizi. She was French, or pretended to be. Her face was very heavily made up and she stood as rigid as a clothing dummy in a display window, unmoving. Only an occasional blinking of her eyes revealed the fact that she was human. The window dresser—a young man with the face of a matinee idol—was removing her garments one by one. The audience watched breathlessly as her breasts came into view, then the slim, stockinged legs.

While the window dresser went to another part of the dais and arranged the summer garments in which he was to dress her, the mannikin came to life, moving in jerky motions, eyes blinking animatedly. Her face registered surprise as she touched her rigid breasts, the smoothness of her bare thighs. Fear and delight crossed her waxen features. No longer was she a mannikin but a living person!

When the window dresser turned back, the dummy froze, motionless.

But now as the young man began to dress her, his fingers found that her flesh was soft and warm, no longer hard and cold. Surprise held him, and an impish delight made him grin.

He ventured to stroke the smooth flesh of her hip and thigh. The mannikin gave a shudder.

Turning her head gently—Zizi made it seem that she was still a thing of cotton and wires and fabric—he kissed her lips. Jerkily the dummy raised an arm to his shoulder. As if life flowed into her body slowly, she began to respond to his caresses. Little by little the automaton disappeared and the living girl emerged. Now she clung to the young man, kissing him feverishly, letting him lift and carry her across the dais to the couch where her discarded garments had been tossed. She helped him sweep them to the floor then lay back and held out her arms. Quickly, then, the lights winked out.

When the gas lamps flared on again, the stage was empty. Applause exploded. Men whistled and stamped their feet. The wine girls came running to pour d'Yquem and Montrachet and to have their buttocks pinched and patted. At a rear table, well hidden by shadows, Moira Creegan sat with her hands closed about a brandy snifter. Her eyes were bright and alert.

Thirty tables—thirty thousand dollars locked in her safe. The Upstairs Club had been an inspiration. She had a waiting list of another dozen names, too. Perhaps, during the summer, she might redecorate and enlarge the room. Forty-two thousand dollars was a lot more than thirty. In two years she would have paid back the sixty thousand it cost to buy off The Egyptian and she would have a profit, besides.

The gaslights lowered to permit girl slaves in papier-mâché manacles to carry an easel, a painter's table and a studio chair to the dais. For a switch, the model was to be a handsome young man, the artist, an attractive girl. It was a skit designed to revive jaded appetites, as were all the shows enacted on the velvet dais. The heavy-set, wealthy men seated with their mistresses or other friends at the tables, demanded forbidden entertainment of this sort; it was the reason why they parted with a thousand dollars so willingly; they knew Moira Creegan, knew the sort of entertainment she would give them.

She smiled coldly in the darkness.

It was an easy way to grow rich, certainly. The men and girls who pantomimed their stage roles were well paid, and had no objections to acting out the parts assigned them. They all knew that along Canal Street, anything went.

116

Penny Drayman had talked her into also adding another sideline to the main business of The Golden Tassel. The canal captains who rode the waterway between Albany and Buffalo would pay good money for pretty cooks. At a price, Moira Creegan would rent them cooks. Once on the canal boats, what the girls did was no concern of hers, and if they came back far richer than they left, the money belonged to them. Girls from other establishments along Big Ditch Street flocked to The Golden Tassel to be hired.

It was as a canal-boat cook that Dottie Alford had met and become engaged to Bill Candell. Their wedding was to take place on the stage of The Golden Tassel three Sundays from now. The Tassel would be closed, of course, except to special, invited guests. The house was open to them as Moira Creegan's wedding present.

Moira wondered if Kathleen would ever know that her mother was doing to guarantee her future happiness. God! If ever she learned, her world—the world built so painstakingly on ruthlessness and immorality—would come crashing down in shards. No, Kathleen must never know. And she would not know. There was no one to betray Moira Creegan.

Not even Mike Gannon. Mike continued to see Kathy, bringing her presents, taking her out to dinner at times. Though she hated him for his faithlessness to her, Moira admitted that his visits to Kathy pleased her. At first she had tried to deny him to her daughter, but Kathy would have none of it. "I love Uncle Mike and I'm going to see him whether you like it or not. I look on him as—as my father." Moira had stormed and wept but when Kathleen pinned her down for reasons to justify her sudden animosity, she realized she could not betray Mike without also betraying herself.

And so, while Kathleen grew into young womanhood—she would be fifteen in another few days—she had her mother and her Uncle Mike to share her days and a few of her evenings. She was doing well in school, so well that Moira was determined to send her to France to complete her education. She would be able to afford it. The Upstairs Club alone would more than pay for it in a single year, once the mortgage to Frank Bannerman was redeemed.

A footfall sounded behind Moira. Penelope Drayman was bending toward her, wearing her costume for the third act, a transparent nightgown and negligee.

"We've got troubles with Dottie. She's having hysterics."

Moira came off her chair with a rustle of taffeta undergarments. Fright caught her in a cold grip. Not another Pamela Travis. Oh, dear God—not that!

CHAPTER NINE

Dottie Alford was a crumpled ball of misery in the tiny dressing room down the hall from The Upstairs Club. Her mascara and make-up had run so that she looked like a caricature of the woman of fashion she was dressed to represent. She was moaning and sobbing uncontrollably. Even when Moira put a hand on her shoulder and shook her, she only wailed more loudly.

"I'm going to kill myself! I'll kill myself! I will! I will!"

"Stop it, Dottie. Now stop it, do you hear? You're a very lucky girl. You have Bill and—you do have Bill, don't you?"

"Yes—I guess so. But—"

She poured out words between her harsh sobbings. Moira was able to make sense from them, after a while. Dottie had sold the farm to buy a trousseau, giving up her struggle with Bill to get him to move off the canal and to a farm, resigning herself to being without him during the long hauls he would have to make.

"B-but Bill d-didn't know that," she wailed. "He s-sold his b-barge and b-bought all new farm equipment as a s-surprise for me. Oh, I could just die. . ."

"A canal captain without a barge, and farm tools without a farm," said Penny, shrugging. "What a hell of a great start for a married life."

Moira bit her lip, patting Dottie soothingly. "Wait here, honey. I think I can do something about this. Just dry your tears and get ready for your act. Maybe I'll have good news for you."

She would seek out Frank Bannerman. He was a real estate man. If anyone could help, he could. Strange how she always needed a man to lean upon, despite her hunger for independence. First it had been Richard, then Mike. Now it was the Buffalo society man.

Bannerman agreed to work, and work fast.

At the wedding ceremony, Moira was able to hand Dottie and Bill a deed to the farm. "I bought it back as a wedding present for you," she told them, almost smothered by their delighted hugs. "Now get out of here before you have me bawling."

Her girls and The Upstairs Club were her hobbies. The Golden Tassel continued to draw crowds night after night. More and more money went into her parlor safe, to be withdrawn and deposited to her account in the Buffalo Savings Bank. She was so wrapped up in her business dealings that even Kathleen became a stranger to her. The girl was like a living goal she had set herself, not to be enjoyed until it was attained. And she could not obtain Kathleen until she was ready to cut her ties with The Golden Tassel, The Upstairs Club, and Canal Street.

At times, she felt she was on a treadmill. The days and the weeks went by so fast, merging into months and then into years, that she was always a little amazed when she went outside Canal Street to learn how the world was wagging.

There was universal indignation in the air at the proposed Wilson Bill in the United States Congress, designed to institute a personal income tax of two per cent on all earned money above four thousand dollars. Moira was more than indignant, for the thought of giving away two per cent of her income—at a rough guess that might be in the neighborhood of one thousand dollars!—struck her almost speechless. She paid a flying visit to her lawyer in bitter protest, and was assured that the law was being attacked as unconstitutional.

The world was changing all around her.

The bitterest blow of all came with her sudden arrest, a few blocks above The Terrace. It was the morning of the day when Kathleen was to take the train to New York, the first leg of her journey to a girls boarding school in France. Moira had hired a brougham but the brougham had broken a wheel on a cobblestone and now she was forced to walk, hunting for another gig. As she passed The Terrace, she saw a uniformed patrolman stare hard at her, turn and begin to walk in her footsteps. She thought no more about him until he put a hand on her shoulder.

"Hold up, dearie. You come from below The Terrace, don't you? From Canal Street?"

"Well, of course I do," she snapped. "I'm going to—"

"Shop?" he asked with an uptilted eyebrow.

"I'm going to see my daughter off to Europe."

The policeman lost his grin. His hand tightened on the upper sleeve of her fashionable Empire dress. "That's enough sass, you two-bit chippy," he growled, and hustled her ahead of him, hand still gripping her gown, to the Delaware Avenue police station.

She learned too late that a new law had been passed in Buffalo, forbidding a woman of the Canal Street area to come north of The Terrace. She gave her name as Daisy Frost to avoid publicity. If her name ever made the papers as the proprietor of The Golden Tassel, she would lose Kathleen forever. Her daughter would understand no reason strong enough to excuse the sort of life she led.

She refused to seek help from Frank Bannerman or from Brandon Partridge. Cautious inquiries brought her a newspaper in which she read of Kathleen's leaving for New York, and from New York to Havre in a Cunard Line steamship. Mike Gannon —he was a famous man in Buffalo these days, with his fifty-odd canal barges and an expanding transportation empire which now included a dozen Great Lakes freighters—had been there to see her off. Gannon had presented her with a dozen American Beauty roses and a diamond watch, together with a check for five thousand dollars from her mother, who was unavoidably detained in Chicago on business.

Good old Mike. A father, Kathleen had said.

Moira bit her lip and wept.

Thirty days later Moira Creegan walked out of the workhouse with her chin high in the air. Kathleen was in Europe by now. Mike Gannon, the newspapers said, was in Schenectady superintending the building of a new warehouse. Frank Bannerman was in Niagara Falls on a real estate transaction. None of her friends were around to meet her, and her girls dared not come north of The Terrace.

It struck her suddenly that no one—absolutely no one in all Buffalo—had missed her very much. Was she that unimportant? The pride which had been injured so badly during her thirty days in jail flared up again. Frank Bannerman was still in Niagara Falls. When he returned he would be treated to a little surprise.

His mistress would refuse to sleep with him.

"But why?" he wanted to know two weeks later. "What in God's name have I done?"

"You were away," she explained sweetly, "when I needed you."

It did not srike her that she was being unreasonable.

Her moodiness grew in the months that followed. There were entire days when she remained locked in her suite of rooms, seeing no one, not even Penny Drayman. The girls could hear her striding back and forth, sometimes laughing uncontrollably, sometimes weeping in terrible loneliness.

"She misses her daughter," some of the girls said.

Penny disagreed. "The woman is no spring chicken. My guess is her menopause has come. It makes her bitter and angry sometimes, sorrowful and repentant at others, proud and willful the rest of the time. Humor her, everybody."

In her more energetic moments she would fling herself into the running of The Golden Tassel and The Upstairs Club. Her inventive mind planned small orgies for the club members. At times she gave them Roman togas to wear, especially made, and had slave girls chained to the heavy tables for their amusement. She conducted Casanova nights, when the members must wear eighteenth century costumes. Once she ordered that the guests were to appear as Greek and Roman gods, or satyrs and nymphs. The room had been so decorated that it seemed a forest glade. Statues of Priapus and Tutinus decorated the room, together with oil paintings of orgies and bacchanalia.

Some nights when Frank Bannerman came to call he would find the heavy wooden door to her suite locked and bolted. To balance these disappointments, she often waited for him in her big double bed stretched out white and naked and fully receptive to his frenzied love-making. She was at once a challenge and a symbol, and to Frank Bannerman, a succubus who held him in fleshly thralldom.

There were letters from Kathleen every week to lighten the burden of her loneliness, and an occasional tidbit of news from some man who had been to other cities on business.

The Egyptian was in New York City, Moira learned. She had set herself up in business in the West Seventies, and at latest report was making money hand over fist. The news infuriated her and for three days thereafter she was in a savage, morose mood.

Winter fled before spring, and became summer.

Kathleen was visiting with friends on the French Riviera. She wrote that she was happy, meeting fascinating new people, and not to worry, she was not at all homesick. Moira cried for hours over her letter. It was her first realization that Kathleen was growing into a life of her own, that she was no longer a baby, despite the fact that her mother considered her still a child. What struck terror into Moira Creegan was the thought that the letter was an omen of the days that were to come.

Time became an endlessness to the woman who ran The Golden Tassel. She withdrew more and more into the life she had built for herself on Canal Street. Long ago she had taken her things from Bertha Jennings' boarding house. Against the time when Kathleen would return from France, she commissioned Frank Banneramn to find her a fashionable mansion along Niagara Street or Deleware Avenue.

Now she waited, counting the days, until Kathleen came home.

It was Penny Drayman who brought the news, running breathlessly into The Upstairs Club room where Moira was planning a new entertainment for its members. She had to take a deep breath and put a hand to the bodice of her gown before she could speak of the news which so excited her.

"She's back, just as big as life."

"Back? Who's back?"

"Lily Anders! She's taken over Frenchy Duval's old place. She's brought a dozen of her New York girls with her, too. She's setting up a Gold Key Club—copying us!"

"Lily? Back in Buffalo? Why, she only left for New York last year—no, it was longer ago than that. Of course! That was the year. . ."

Her voice trailed off. Four years? Five? Why, it must be all of that. So many things had happened since then! Kathleen was in Europe. Mike Gannon was on his way to becoming a rich man, though she never saw him any more. She herself was now Frank Bannerman's mistress.

She wondered if The Egyptian had come back to make trouble. Then she shrugged; Lily would make no trouble for Moira Creegan she would see to that, since she was so close to quitting The Golden Tassel. She had nothing to gain and everything to lose by reviving her feud with the dusky Anders woman.

Mike Gannon smelled the smoke before he saw it.

He came walking down Big Ditch Street with two of his barge captains at his back. His nostrils twitched and he drew a deep breath, shouting unintelligibly to his men, breaking into a run. As he rounded the corner of his warehouse, he saw the black, billowing clouds rising skyward.

An instant later, flames shot out from five of his newest barges. Even as he pounded across the cobblestones, his mind was alive with suspicion. All five at once? This was no accident. A fire might break out on one barge, though safety rules were enforced from Buffalo to Albany by his captains. But all five?

Others had seen the fires. By the time Gannon was at the pilings, half a dozen fire pumps were in operation. Years before he had insisted that his warehousemen learn to use the hand pumps; now they were paying off for him. Steady streams of water were inundating the newly painted barges. Gusts of steam hissed and swirled through the black smoke as water sprayed the flames.

"Who?" Mike asked bitterly. "Was it Bennett?"

His foreman said, "Joe and Walt saw a man run from the *Lucky Day,* and went after him. Ought to be back by now, if they caught the bastard."

Inaction put an itch deep inside Mike Gannon. He was in his forties, now, but he was a hard man, used to long working hours. He hefted a fire axe and went on board the *Lucky Day.* The damage was not as bad as he had feared. His axe battered down partitions. He roared orders for his men to wheel the hand pump onto the deck.

It took an hour to put all the fires out. By that time Walt and Joe were back, dragging a terrified man between them. To Mike's surprise he was a man he himself had hired two weeks before, named Bertie Farr.

Grime on his face and hands, with his clothes singed from jumping sparks, the big Irishman stood over the seated Farr in his warehouse office. Joe had taken a handful of greenbacks from his pocket. They lay on the foreman's desk.

Mike counted them. "Fifty dollars, you goddamn Judas. Who gave it to you?"

Walt brought the back of a meaty hand across Farr's face. The smaller man whimpered and lifted his arm protectively. "Don't 'it me no more, guv'nor. Didn't want to do it. Man told me I'd get another fifty if I did it right."

123

"A big man with black hair and a gold watch chain across his middle? Red face? Black eyes?"

The small man nodded fearfully. Mike slowly clenched his fists. "Black John himself. I thought those days were over, it's been so peaceful the last eight, nine years." He shot a glance at Walt. "How many boys we got handy?"

"Seven barge crews, loading now. The warehouse gang. A few more hangers-on I give odd jobs to."

Gannon smiled coldly. "Twenty dollars a man for a little fight. Weapons supplied. Tell them that."

Walt whistled softly and turned on his heel with a grin. Things had been too quiet along the Big Ditch lately. A good battle royal was years overdue. And to get paid for swinging a pick handle or a sap! This was a dream come true.

Mike inspected every barge before he was satisfied the fires were out. He came up out of the hold of the *Lucky Day* and he took off his coat and ripped loose his tie. A man needed freedom of movement in a free-for-all. He took the axe handle Walt tossed him, and looked around at the grinning faces.

"I never thought I'd be walking up this street at the head of a small army again," he told them. "I figured those days were all behind me. But if Bennett wants open war we'll give it to him."

They marched as once before they had marched long ago, the tramping of heavy boots behind him worked an echoing thumping in his heart. His fingers tightened on the axe handle.

Half a dozen men were lounging in the Empire Line offices. They took one look at the huge Irishman as his brogan kicked in the office door and fled. The safe was left open. Papers were scattered here and there on desks and filing cabinets.

"Pile 'em up," Mike told his men. "Paper, chairs, desks, everything in the middle of the floor."

He helped until a name written on a ledger sheet caught his eye. Lily Anders. The Egyptian. Now what in the name of God was her name doing in Black John Bennett's account books? He roared a halt to all activity, and directed his men's energy in a hunt for more such ledgers.

It took an hour and a half, but by that time Mike Gannon was armed with all the information he needed. His lips twisted wryly, bitterly, as he wrapped cords about the books he wanted. Then he struck a match and set the rest on fire.

"We'll go on to The Golden Tassel," he told his men. "I've a feeling the man I want to see is somewhere around those premises."

Walt growled, "Empire ought to've showed before now. Isn't like Black John to let us ransack and burn his property without a fight."

Mike chuckled. "Maybe we caught him by surprise. He may be out gathering more men. I hope he is. Sure, it'd be a crying shame if I didn't get to swing this fine new axe handle against at least one Empire skull."

Moira Creegan sat a long time before her vanity mirror staring at the cablegram in her hands. She was trembling fitfully, poised between tears and laughter. Kathleen was coming home! By tomorrow, the train she was taking from New York would pull into the Lehigh Valley depot.

She bowed her head, putting both hands to her cheeks, and wept with happiness. "I can't believe it. I just can't believe it," she whispered.

Frank Bannerman came from the washroom in his shirt-sleeves, toweling his hands. "It means the end of The Golden Tassel and The Upstairs Club, of course," he said. "You'll have to go into retirement."

Her head lifted. "Have I enough money, Frank? Have I?"

"Close to a million dollars, at last count. Isn't that enough to satisfy you?"

"Yes, I suppose so."

"Invested wisely, it will grow. I've gone over business opportunities with you. First mortgages. Stock issues. Certain bonds. You can increase your wealth, Moira. You don't have to turn into a little old lady just because you're leaving all this behind you." His hand made a motion around the ornate bedroom.

He came up behind her, smiling down into her eyes. "You're still a very attractive woman. You could even marry if you wanted. I'd marry you in the morning if—if it weren't for my own wife."

"You could never divorce her, could you, Frank?"

"It just isn't done in our set. Besides, she's a very wealthy woman. She's made me rather independent of business collapses and bear markets." He shook out his cuffs. "Divorce? I think not. If she died—but why bother with wishes?"

"Why bother?" she wondered, and swung around to face the vanity mirrors. Frank was right. She was still a handsome woman. In the silk peignoir she could study her body at leisure. Her breasts were still firm, thank heaven! Her waist was small and her legs, though heavier with the years, were as curved and shapely as ever. She extended a foot and turned it, studying the white thigh and rounded calf.

"I don't know any man I'd marry right now," she said. "But there's always someone waiting to be found, I suppose."

His face clouded. He put hands on her shoulders.

"Moira, I wish you wouldn't do any—"

An explosion of sound swung them toward the bedroom doorway. Moira gathered her wrapper tighter about her body and moved into the front parlor. A voice was shouting from below stairs, a male voice and an angry one.

"Who in the world?" she wondered, and went to the hall door. Hard, jarring footsteps sounded in the corridor. Suddenly indignant, she yanked open the door.

Mike Gannon stood before her, half a dozen ledgers and account books under an arm. "Faith now, it's the lady herself. It's glad I am to see you."

"Mike! Have you gone mad? Get out of here."

"Ah, no. Not so fast, my fine lady. Not until I've had my little say with you." Mike turned as Frank Bannerman came into the room, puzzled and vaguely alarmed. "Good afternoon, sir. You stay long in bed, it seems."

Mike walked past Moira as if she did not exist. He put his account books down on the parlor table, turned and walked up to the society man. "You've had a lot of fun at my expense through the years, haven't you, Bannerman? Hiding out behind Black John Bennett and Lily Anders."

His hand lifted. The back of it went crashing across Bannerman's face, knocking the man backwards. Moira screamed and ran to Mike, hammering at his hard chest with tiny fists. "What goes on in that crazy head of yours, anyhow?"

His glance raked her white body, naked under the peignoir. "I loved you once. Maybe I still love you, God forgive me. Anyhow, I thought you might like to know a few things about this gentleman friend of yours."

Bannerman was in the doorway, a handkerchief pressed to his bleeding mouth. His eyes were bright black pools of fury above his bruised cheeks. "Gannon, I'll see you dead for this. I—"

126

Mike laughed at him. "Ah, will you? Faith, you give me the excuse I've been hankering for and not finding, this past half hour." He went up to Bannerman, caught him by his shirt front and the jacket of his coat, and drove a huge fist into his face.

"This is for all the trouble you've caused me in the past ten, twelve years, you sneaking bastard. At least Black John is man enough to admit he hates my guts and has tried to settle matters between us man-to-man."

The fist hit, and hit again. Moira was screaming, hands to her cheeks, staring with bulging eyes as Mike Gannon broke the other man's nose and blacked his eyes. Bannerman tried to fight back but he was no match for the big Irishman. After a while Mike flung him across the room to collapse on the thick Turkish carpet.

"Mike, I swear to God I'll—"

"Spare me your curses! Come and have a look at this ledger book."

"I won't look at anything you have to show me."

Mike grinned coldly. "Not even if I tell you that ever since you bought out The Egyptian you've been working to put money in her pockets?"

Moira stared at him, horrified. "Now I know you're mad!"

"Am I? Don't be too sure. See here—"

He opened an account book and held it toward her. Moira looked at him very steadily, trying to read his hard blue eyes, before she lowered her gaze to the ledger sheet. A moment she read, then gasped and swayed.

"A transfer of a half interest in The Golden Tassel rentals to Lily Anders. You'll note the date, my love. Before your agreement with her to end your partnership."

"I don't understand," she whispered.

"Oh, now! Use your brains. Frank Bannerman owned The Golden Tassel before the date of the agreement written down here. Suddenly he gives a half interest to The Egyptian. Why, in Christ's name—*except that he was paying her off?*"

"Paying Lily off? For what?"

Mike dropped the ledger. His fingers went into the soft flesh of her upper arms. "For playing a love scene with me the night you walked in and found us in the Morris chair. Ah, your Frankie is a smart one. He had everything worked out to a fine point. I'm back from Albany hungering for your

127

love, ripe to the point of exploding. Lily walks into this room in little more than you're wearing yourself, right now."

He groaned. "I'm not excusing myself. I'm guilty as hell. I admit it. I've paid a price for my guilt, though. But the whole thing wouldn't have happened if Lily hadn't been working for your precious Bannerman at the moment."

The society man was standing, swaying drunkenly. Mike pointed a finger at him. "Deny it, you bastard. Also deny if you can the fact that you've been a silent partner of Black John Bennett for upwards of twenty years. You and Bennett own the Empire Line together. You're as guilty as Bennett for burning my five barges today."

"Burning your barges? You're crazy. I distinctly told Bennett not to—" He paused stricken, as Mike chuckled.

"You're the reason for the truce between us, then? Soon as you got your hands on Moira here, you told Bennett to lay off me. You didn't want Moira feeling sorry for me."

He swung on Moira angrily, flinging out a hand toward Bannerman. Moira was backing away from them both, fingers pressing into her cheeks, staring from one man to the other. Revulsion and shame tinted her face and throat a dull red.

"To think I trusted—"

The sound of a rock crashing through window glass brought her up short. She turned, staring. Below in the street they could hear the high-pitched scream of an angry woman. Moira ran to a curtained window and drawing back the white cretonne, stared down at the cobblestoned stretch of Canal Street. Mike came and stood behind her. After one glance at them, Bannerman went to the other window.

A woman in a black taffeta gown and a red pelisse was facing the front of The Golden Tassel. From the front doorway of The Golden Tassel, Penny Drayman ran to meet her. They slammed together in the middle of the street, fists flailing and fingers curved to claw. Penny locked a hand in the elaborate coiffure of the New York girl, hauling back, reaching with her left hand for the girl's cheeks.

Two more New York women came on the run. They fell on Penny Drayman and began to kick and scratch. One of them fastened both hands in her dress and ripped it down the back. Penny was exposed in red-and-white striped corset and long red silk stockings. Instantly the three New York women began to maul and gouge her revealed flesh. They

128

could hear her screams of agony even through the closed windows.

Then half a dozen girls came out of The Golden Tassel. They caught the three New Yorkers and began fighting viciously, panting and cursing obscenely. More of The Egyptian's entertainers ran from the Gold Key Club. Moira saw her own girls hurry to meet them. In seconds the street was filled with scratching, pummeling women.

Mike said, "Now look who's coming!"

Black John Bennett was striding down Canal Street. A small mob of Empire Line roustabouts walked at his back, armed with pick handles and axes, the necks of broken bottles, knives and leather-covered saps. The Lucky Line men who had followed Mike Gannon to The Golden Tassel thrust away from the walls of the buildings where they had been loafing, laughing and egging on the girls.

Mike whirled and grabbed the society man by the lapels of his suit jacket. "Here they come, you conniving bastard! Your men. And your toady, Black John. For once, you're going to be in the thick of the same fight I am!"

He drew back his fist and drove it hard against Bannerman's jaw. Blood spouted from his crushed nose. The society man tried to fight back. He picked up a lamp and hurled it. Glass shattered and kerosene sprayed the rug and furniture. His hand went out for his cane. A wrench of his wrist and a length of cold steel slid into view.

"A sword cane," grunted Mike, and laughed harshly. "All right, you son of a bitch! If you want to play it this way."

His own big hands went out to catch up a bronze statuette. Gannon hurled it. Bannerman dodged, but not quickly enough. The heavy metal caught him in the shoulder and half-turned him. In that moment Gannon dove over the library table, scattering lamps and magazines. His fingers fastened on the cane wrist of the society man and his shoulder barreled into his chest.

Bannerman went hard into the wall. Mike drove a big fist deep into his mid-section. The breath wheezing out of his lungs made a whistling sound. When he let him go, Bannerman sank to the floor, broken and bleeding. Mike picked up the sword cane and snapped its blade over the edge of the heavy oak library table.

Moira followed his every move with bulging eyes.

Mike growled, "Here's your man, Moira darling. Now

129

you'll have to excuse me. Black John will be looking for me down there on the street."

Moira smiled faintly as she shrugged out of her silk peignoir. "Wait for me, Mike Gannon. Today it's Buffalo against New York. You say Black John is looking for you? I think Lily Anders will be hunting for me. If she isn't, I'm going to search for her!"

Mike drew a deep breath, seeing this woman standing naked before him. She ran into the bedroom and through the open door he could see her slipping on a corset, pulling a bombazine dress down over her head, wriggling her hips to to smooth it out.

When she was ready she turned to Mike. "All right. I'm ready."

"Moira, you stay here! It makes no difference if the police come for me during the fight. But—"

She ran ahead of him into the hall and stood there, breathing fitfully. "Are you coming? Or am I going out there alone?"

He ran after her and, side by side, they pounded down the hall and to the wide, curving staircase and then through The Golden Tassel out onto the cobblestones of Big Ditch Street. The fight had spread up and down the block. Black John and his Empire bunch were driving back the Lucky Line canawlers. The Egyptians and her New Yorkers were getting the better of The Golden Tassel girls.

Mike spit on his hands and rubbed them together. "All right, Moira Kennally. You wanted a fight. Here's one made to order for you!"

Moira reached down and tore her skirt at its seams, giving her legs freedom to run. Then she moved forward slowly, tearing the sleeves from her dress. Her eyes hunted for The Egyptian but could not find her.

Instead she leaped into a knot of girls surrounding Zizi and Hortense. Her fists thudded into soft flesh. Two girls went down before her. The bombazine dress was ripped to her navel and her breasts shook free of the fabric, but she was far beyond modesty. A tall redhead from New York was coming for her with a piece of broken glass in a hand. Moira went off her feet in a low dive, hitting the girl below her knees, taking her legs out from under her.

As she landed, Moira whirled. Her hands sank deep into thick red hair. Lifting the girl's head, she began to pound it up and down on a cobblestone.

Mike Gannon had picked up an axe handle seconds before he threw himself into the battle. Now he lifted and swung it again and again, delighting in the shock of contact. His voice roared incoherently but his men caught its sound and found new spirit in their tired arms and battered bodies.

The axe handle he wielded like a sword, banging heads and faces until he cleared a path for himself and the men who formed a wedge at his back. His heavy brogans were slipping and sliding on unconscious men who had fallen at the first onslaught. As he fought, his eyes hunted for Black John Bennett. Not finding him, he roared the louder and fought the harder, hoping that Bennett would hear and seek him out.

The handle was red with blood but still Gannon whipped it back and forth. The Empire men had begun to buckle. Sensing victory, Mike bellowed, urging his men to further efforts. He drove them as he drove the length of wood in his hand. He whipped them to an angry pitch with his voice and brought them fighting in his wake.

His left hand caught a man and whirled him out of his path. The axe handle caught another across the back of the neck, pitching him senseless underfoot. A third rose up and suddenly Mike found himself staring at Black John Bennett.

His shirt had long ago been ripped to shredded cloth so that half of his hairy chest was bare, with trickles of blood running down it. They pitched away axe handle and leaden sap, and came together with clenched fists. Bennett landed first, a straight left that rocked the big Irishman back on his heels. Black John came forward roaring triumph, but Mike swung a left hook to his jaw and a right to his midsection to bring him up short. Then they flung themselves forward at the same time, meeting with fists driving into bruised and bleeding flesh, feet slipping on the wet cobbles, grunting and cursing with hate and a cold, terrible anger.

His body was moving, hitting and dodging, but Mike found himself thinking that all his troubles might well be blamed on this man who stood before him. Ah, and Frank Bannerman, too, but the real estate man lay broken and unconscious in an upstairs room of The Golden Tassel. He had settled his accounts, in a way, with Bannerman. His score with Bennett still needed to be taken care of.

And so he neither felt the blows he took, nor the jarring impact of the clouts he was hammering at Black John. He stood suspended in a little world where he was repaying this man for the heartache of the years. Bennett and Bannerman were partners, and because Bannerman had made him lose Moira Creegan, so now he blamed Black John for his loss as well.

Moira Creegan was flat on her back when she saw The Egyptian. Two of the New York girls had caught her by the hair and an arm and yanked her backwards. She landed hard on the cobblestones and was stretched out fighting for breath when Lily Anders came leaping for her, a high-heeled shoe raised to dig into her chest. Moira rolled over and came to her knees. The Egyptian had halted her foot in midkick. Now she swung a rock in her right hand straight for Moira's head.

Moira lunged forward, taking the rock on a shoulder but getting both hands on the left leg of The Egyptian, where it was exposed through the strips of her ripped dress. Moira opened her mouth and lunged.

Her teeth sank deep in The Egyptian's thigh, some pagan part of her exulting in the screech Lily loosed at that savage bite. This dusky woman had flaunted her nakedness before her Mike. With her womanly wiles she had seduced him. At the moment, she did not hate Mike Gannon. He was a man, and weak where a woman was concerned. The Egyptian knew Mike Gannon belonged to Moira Creegan. She had deliberately set out to win him away from her.

Moira bit again, and now she felt Lily tumbling sideways, fingers reaching for Moira's long black hair. A sharp tug thrust agony through the scalp yet she delighted in the pain. It roused her fury even further. Now her hands were long-nailed claws ripping the exposed areas of the other woman's body.

They rolled over and over across the cobblestones, kicking, raking one another with sharp fingernails. Blood ran redly from The Egyptian's naked thighs. Moira Creegan found her left eye was puffed and rapidly closing, making vision difficult. She clung to Lily, not daring to let go of her, afraid she might not be able to find her again once they were parted.

Slowly she crawled on top of the other woman. Her rage was a pounding aliveness in her heart. Her head rang with it. She bent and bit and gloried in the scream she heard. Now The Egyptian was babbling, crying out, trying to escape the woman who clung to her, the fight gone out of her before the pain that ran all along her veins.

"Let go," she screamed. "Christ, Moira—you're killing me! Oh my God—stop! Stop!"

"Frank Bannerman hired you to seduce Mike Gannon, didn't he?" Moira sobbed bitterly. "He paid you and you took his money like the whore you are!"

"Yes, yes, yes. It's all true but—stop biting me. I can't stand—that any—more!"

Moira clenched both hands in The Egyptian's hair. She straddled her, legs naked to her hips, sobbing fiercely, "You were to make sure I caught you together, weren't you? Damn you, Lily—answer me!"

She began to pound the head up and down against the cobblestones. She was whispering curses and screaming obscenities when a coarse blue sleeve caught her around the neck and dragged her back. She would not release her hold on the unconscious Egyptian's hair until a police nightstick beat down on her wrists.

Panting heavily, Moira put a hand to her fallen hair, lifting it out of her eyes. A score of Deleware Avenue patrolmen were moving in and out of the melee, using their clubs, separating those groups of men and women who were still battling. As her vision cleared a little, she began to recognize policemen from outlying precincts.

"More'n three-quarters of the whole damned force is down here today," a police captain told her. "The whole city's in an uproar."

Moira staggered drunkenly toward the paddy wagon as a hand gripped her upper arm, urging her along. Suddenly the hand went away and as Moira turned, she saw Black John Bennett reeling wildly under a flood of hammering blows that ripped into him from belt to forehead. She gasped when she saw Mike, bloody and with most of his clothes torn away. One foot was shod, the other was bare. Dark bruises ran over his entire body, from head to chest. His ankle was bleeding where a broken bottle had cut it. Someone had slashed his calf with a knife.

Seven policemen had to drag him away from Bennett, who fell face down on the cobblestones and lay unmoving. Mike tried to fight the police, not knowing who they were, but half a dozen billies crashed into the back of his head. He stood like a great tree an instant before its felling by a timberjack. Then he toppled, face down, onto the cobblestone, right at Moira's feet.

She stared down at him, her heart overflowing. Realization had come to her at last—on this long, bitter afternoon on Canal Street—that this man was her life. For years she had fought the sensual appeal he had for her body. She had siphoned off the love she bore for him to Kathleen, to The Golden Tassel, to her girls. She had been afraid to yield to him completely.

Now she went to her knees in the dirt and blood of the street. She lifted his head and rested it on a scratched and bleeding white thigh. Her hands soothed back the thick, graying black hair from his forehead.

At her touch, his eyes flickered open. "Moira, mavourneen. It was a grand fight while it lasted but—Jesus! The last time Bennett hit me he almost tore my head off."

Moira wept and laughed. "It was seven coppers hitting you at once with their nightsticks, darling."

"You called me darling?"

She bit her lip, not caring suddenly that her cheeks were wet with tears, and that her love for this big man was suddenly singing through her veins until she wanted to lie right down on the cobblestones and make love to him. Then rough hands were under her arms, raising her up, hurrying her toward the paddy wagon. Her last sight of Mike Gannon showed him struggling weakly in the hands of four burly officers, being dragged into a waiting Black Maria.

Then she saw The Egyptian, almost naked and still out cold, being lifted and put in still a third police van. There must be a dozen of them, she realized suddenly, staring around her out of puffy eyes.

Almost every precinct in Buffalo had a wagon here.

It had been a fight to make history.

CHAPTER TEN

A single gas lamp burned in the dim room.

Outside, dusk layered the city of Buffalo in a dark haze. For hours Moira Creegan had been standing at the window, staring out over the rooftops. There was no life in her, though her heart still beat and her eyes still saw.

Only yesterday, here in this room and down there on the cobblestones, she had been a living, breathing woman. There

134

had been no thought of death in her then. She had been vital, alive. Those few moments when she had held Mike Gannon in her arms had seemed to be the start of a new, better life for her.

Even when the paddy wagon had carted her off to the police station, to spend the night behind bars until Partridge, Heap and Taggart could sent a clerk down with bail money, she had not fully understood how her world was ending. Only this morning, when the newspapers had appeared. . . .

They lay scattered across the library table, mute testimony to the despair now freezing her veins. All day long she had gone without food, reading those accounts over and over again. Her incredulous eyes had tried to blot out the picture some zealous newspaper photographer had made of her being escorted into the jail yard with a patrolman hanging onto each arm.

Moira Creegan, madame of a bawdy house on Canal Street, being taken from the police van to a jail cell. Mrs. Creegan is the proprietress of one of the most notorious houses on Canal Street, The Golden Tassel.

The caption writers and the rewrite men had enjoyed a field day. She could quote the editorial accompanying the photograph from memory.

The police bagged a big one yesterday after the riot along Big Ditch Street. Moira Creegan herself, with hair disarranged and her garments almost torn from her body, was drawn in by the police net. With her capture, the spirit of the battle royal was broken. Never before has any girl from The Golden Tassel, much less its notorious madame, been guilty of so flagrant a violation of the law.

It is high time that public-minded citizens rally to the challenge these bold women pose. Rumor says that within The Golden Tassel is a still more vicious bordello called The Upstairs Club, where vice is sold on the grand scale—

A sob broke from her lungs. She buried her face in her hands. All this was bad enough, but early this morning, Kathleen had arrived at the Lehigh Valley depot. She should have been there to meet her, but she was still in jail.

Kathleen would have had plenty of time to read the papers. By now the mother would have no secrets from the daughter. Moira Creegan, brothel keeper. A woman who sells vice to the rich men of the city of Buffalo. A vicious, evil parasite who deserves only to be stamped out of existence.

Her gaze ranged Canal Street. There were few gaslights this evening after the battle. Its combatants were scattered, nursing their wounds. The Egyptian was in the hospital, under arrest. Penny Drayman was in a cot not far away, also under arrest. She had not heard anything about Mike Gannon, though she supposed he had raised bail, too.

Yesterday, she'd been ready to tell Mike that, if he'd have her, she would marry him. Now that the papers had come out, that was an impossibility. What man wants the fact that his wife had been a brothel keeper to be known to the world?

She could not marrry Mike—and she could not go to her daughter.

No one wanted Moira Creegan. She was a pariah, an outcast. The Golden Tassel was no longer a home. Her girls were scattered, her clientele in hiding in their fine mansions, afraid for their reputations. Everything for which she had worked so hard and so long had been swept away in a few short hours.

Somewhere a church bell bonged the time of services.

Her hand fell away and let the curtain drop. She turned her eyes around the room, seeing the Belter sofa and the thick Turkish rugs, the console table and wall mirror, the crocheted antimacassars on the stuffed chairs and chair bolsters, Sinumbra lamps and glass-domed shell ornaments, as if for the last time. This had been her home, these few rooms here at The Golden Tassel. It seemed she knew no other.

The rooms, like The Golden Tassel itself, would be taken away from her. No longer could she keep up her role of traveling businesswoman. No longer could she remain here, for Brandon Partridge had informed her that the city of Buffalo, aroused by the riot on Canal Street, was preparing to make laws to wipe away the brothels and the entertainment palaces.

No one to have her, nowhere to go. Her life was ended.

Like an already dead person she moved for the last time across the parlor into her bedroom, and through the bedroom to the washroom. In a standing cabinet she kept a few medicines. There was also a bottle of iodine for occasional cuts.

She stood a long time staring at the bottle of iodine before lifting it out of the cabinet and unfastening its stopper. The pungent smell of the liquid touched her nostrils and she wondered if this kind of death would hurt. She hoped not. She had always hated pain.

Swiftly she lifted the bottle to her lips.

Kathleen was sobbing softly as the brougham rattled over the cobblestones. She sat huddled in a corner of the cab wiping at wet eyes while Mike Gannon stared uncomfortably out the window.

"How could she?" she wailed.

The Big Irishman shrugged uncomfortably. His left eye still throbbed with a dull ache where his cheekbone had stopped an axe handle in full swing. Under his blue serge suit his ribs were bandaged tightly. It hurt him to move, even to breathe, yet he had insisted that he come down here to Big Ditch Street with Kathleen. There was a need in him as poignant as there was in the girl.

Yesterday afternoon, when he had opened his eyes to the sight of Moira Creegan bending tenderly above him, he'd understood that he'd come to the end of the trail. He saw the love for him shining in her eyes. The tip of his tongue was already asking her to marry him when those bluecoats had yanked them apart.

What he'd had no time to do yesterday, he'd do today.

"How could she think I'd be anything but grateful f-for everything she's done?" the girl asked. "Does s-she think I'm such a-an ungrateful hussy I'd turn my back on her n-now?"

Mike cleared his throat. "Well now, acushla—your mother gets funny ideas sometimes. But I thought I'd better see you as soon as those newspapers came out. I didn't know what you might be thinking."

She reached for his hand and held it, smiling tremulously. "I'm glad you came, Daddy Mike. I guess I needed somebody to open my eyes to what a wonderful mother I've got."

"Sure, you can tell her that yourself any second now," he said, peering out the window. "We're here at last."

He handed her down on the Canal Street cobblestones. Kathleen looked about her curiously at the shattered windows, the bits of broken bottles, the splintered pick and axe handles, the spots of dried blood that showed where the riot had raged so recently. She shivered. Mike put an arm protectingly about her shoulders, leading her up the stairs and into the cool quiet of The Golden Tassel.

The emptiness of the big room struck at them both. Mike

growled, "Looks like a mausoleum, fit only for the dead."

Their shoes made faint echoes on the wide stairway. Then they were in the upper hall and moving toward the suite of rooms at the far end, the walls of which adjoined the smaller Mummy Case. The door of the parlor was ajar.

Mike pushed it in.

Kathleen ran ahead of him into the bedroom. Mike could hear the faint drumming of her feet on the carpeted floor.

"Mother!"

The stark horror in her young voice lifted Mike to a run. He came through the bedroom door to the sound of scuffling and sobbing in the bathroom. He leaped forward to discover Moira and Kathleen locked in a struggle for a small brown bottle.

The hairs at the back of his neck lifted when he recognized what the bottle contained. "Glory be to God," he breathed, and reached out.

At the touch of his hands, the fight went out of Moira Creegan. She fell back against the wall, staring at him, then at Kathleen "Why weren't you a few minutes later? Why? Why?" she moaned.

Mike turned and hurled the bottle across the bedroom. It hit the far wall and shattered, blotching the wallpaper with brown stains. Then he swung on Moira, face black with fury.

"You ought to be ashamed of yourself, Moira Kennally! What in the name of God's got into you? I'm thinking you don't deserve such a wonderful girl as Kathleen here. If you could have heard how proud she was of you—yes, and how angry that you'd think her ashamed of you—"

Moira turned amazed eyes toward her daughter. Kathleen sobbed softly and fell into her arms. They clung, weeping, while Mike cleared his throat and looked at the washbasin, then studied the white ceiling and the bathtub fixtures.

"Mother, do you think it matters to me if—"

"I was so afraid. And ashamed!"

"You did what you did for me. You gave up everything you'd ever known to make sure I'd never have to do the things you had to do. You sent me to France. You fought to keep me when you could so easily have left me behind in Rome—or let Aunt Martha and Elvira take me back in that lawsuit!"

"I never thought you'd—"

"Mother, I *love* you! When one person loves another it

138

doesn't make any difference what they've been. Can't you understand that?"

Mike growled, "The girl's right, damn it!"

Moira looked at him and now he could see the love gleaming in her eyes as it had gleamed yesterday afternoon; an exultation leaped inside him. He took one step forward and put his arms around the woman he loved, and the girl he loved as a daughter.

"Faith, mavourneen. I'm going to ask you once again— will you marry me?"

"Yes, Mike—oh, yes. Yes!"

Kathleen was laughing through the tears in her eyes. "Have you no manners, either of you?"

They paid her no mind, and so the girl slipped out from between them, giving room Mike room to put arms around her mother and draw her in close to him. Then they were kissing, and Kathleen smiled and turned her back and moved through the bedroom into the parlor.

"I'll wait here," she called.

"No need for that," Mike boomed triumphantly.

He came walking toward her with his arm about her mother's waist. Moira was laughing, flushing faintly, leaning against him languidly. Then Mike put his other arm about Kathleen. Like that they moved out into the hall, walking side by side away from the past into their new future.

The End